Sea Dogs

SEA DOGS

STORIES BY

John Bensko

Graywolf Press

SAINT PAUL, MINNESOTA

Publication of this volume is made possible in part by a grant provided by the Minnesota State Arts Board, through an appropriation by the Minnesota State Legislature; a grant from the Wells Fargo Foundation Minnesota; and a grant from the National Endowment for the Arts. Significant support has also been provided by the Bush Foundation; Target, Marshall Field's and Mervyn's with support from the Target Foundation; the McKnight Foundation; and other generous contributions from foundations, corporations, and individuals. To these organizations and individuals we offer our heartfelt thanks.

Special funding for this title has been provided by the Jerome Foundation.

MINNESOTA
STATE ARTS BOARD

NATIONAL
ENDOWMENT
FOR THE ARTS

Published by Graywolf Press
2402 University Avenue, Suite 203
Saint Paul, Minnesota 55114
All rights reserved.

www.graywolfpress.org

Published in the United States of America

ISBN 1-55597-399-X

2   4   6   8   9   7   5   3   1
First Graywolf Printing, 2004

Library of Congress Control Number: 2003112160

Cover design: Christa Schoenbrodt, Studio Haus

Cover photograph: Craig Brabson

Acknowledgments

Some of the stories in *Sea Dogs*
first appeared in the following:

Chariton Review, "Painted Animals"

Chelsea, "A Spell"

The Georgia Review, "Sea Dogs"

The Greensboro Review, "Sirens"

Kansas Quarterly/Arkansas Review, "A Cabin in the Woods"

The Madison Review, "The Robber"

New England Review, "Tequila Worms"

New Letters, "Creeping Things"

Quarterly West, "Out from Guadalajara"

Sonora Review, "The Ocean"

The Southern Review, "The Palm and the Cat"

Southwest Review, "Summer Girls"

for Cary

Contents

3   Painted Animals

23   The Ocean

37   Summer Girls

51   Tequila Worms

63   Creeping Things

77   Sirens

87   A Spell

101   The Robber

109   Flying St. Croix

131   The Palm and the Cat

147   A Cabin in the Woods

157   Out from Guadalajara

171   Sea Dogs

Sea Dogs

Painted Animals

She had told him they should never live in concrete block, but when she arrived on the bus from Ann Arbor and he took her to the house he'd rented, it was white stucco over block, in a low place under big oaks with Spanish moss hanging from their knotted fairy-tale limbs.

"Isn't it great?" he said, pulling into the sandy drive, veering around the puddles from an early afternoon rain. She'd heard from a friend who had lived in north Florida for years that the rains this time of winter would go on for days. Her friend recalled staring out the window, the sound of steady rain inside her ears a thrumming she couldn't shake.

Janice looked at the dripping trees and at the line of green mold that had crept up the side of the house like the wave mark of an invisible ocean. In one of her stories, she would have put a sad girl in the house and would have had her climb one of the trees one day, finding an old woman who lived in a hole in the trunk. The woman would have told the girl a secret about the place. It would have changed everything.

But as she got out of the car and her foot plunged into a sandy puddle she knew that, secret or no secret, the girl would have slipped on her way down the tree and broken her neck.

"I can't believe you," she said to him. "I told you I didn't want concrete block."

He was unloading her suitcases from the trunk of the car. "Will you get this, honey?" he said, motioning with his shoulder to the trunk lid while he came around the side, a suitcase in each hand.

"Pete, did you hear me?" Her wet shoe sloshing, she went back and slammed down the lid.

"I heard. There's nothing we can do now. It's only for four months. I tried the best I could. This is the way they build things down here." He put the suitcases on the cement landing in front of the door and fumbled for the key. He was boyish, hunched over, his hands in his pockets in front of the screen door. He was still the little boy in the woods she had written about in a story, the child who couldn't find his name.

"There's a great lake near here," he said. "It's called Lake Ella and it has ducks and geese. You'll love it. We can walk there." He found the keys and opened the door, turning toward her as if he were waiting and wouldn't move until he was sure she was going into the house with him. She stayed by the car, her arms crossed in front of her, self-conscious about the pose but determined to keep it.

"I'm not setting foot," she said, "until you tell me why."

"Why what?"

"Why you did it when you knew I didn't want you to."

"It's a dry house," he said. "It's perfectly dry. That was what you were worried about, wasn't it? I swear it's dry."

Standing on one foot, she reached down and loosened her wet shoe, letting the water drain from the heel.

"I had to take it," he said. "It was the only place I could find that would give a six-month lease."

She shook her head. "I'll come in and look around," she said. "But I know it's going to depress me."

Oddly, though, when she walked into the living room she was not at all depressed. At the back of the house, a picture window facing south filled the room with light. There seemed to be more sun inside the house than there had been in the yard, which didn't make sense when she thought about it, but which she accepted, even a little pleased that there was something magical about the place.

"There's a terrific room for you to write in," he said, and he took her hand, leading her down the hall and past the bedroom, the bathroom, into a small room on the southwest corner of the house. It must have once been a child's, with a parade of painted animals around the wall. Turtles, and alligators, and leaping fish. The window shaped the sunlight into a rectangular spot on one big alligator who had his arms spread and his mouth open as if singing. The painting, like the others, struck her as a little crude. The alligator's snout was foreshortened badly, the lower jaw more like a beak. The teeth were the same size in the front as the back, so that they filled the alligator's throat.

Still, crude as they were, the paintings gave her a pleasant feeling. She could picture her writing table under the window, and her couch, the ragged green one she liked to lie on when she was tired and needed to think, along the wall near the door.

Two days later, when the truck with their furniture arrived, she'd decided she'd been wrong to give him such a hard time. They'd spent the nights on sleeping bags on the floor of the living room where the carpet was thicker. It was very romantic. He'd gone out and bought candles and put them on paper plates, even though the electricity had already been connected. The candle-light flickering on the white cement walls softened them, and though no rain fell those two nights she wished it had so she could have heard it dripping off the eaves.

All the furniture had come in, remarkably, without loss, the driver and his assistant unloading quickly, the numbered cardboard cubes resting on the carpet like markers in a game. She enjoyed having so many spaces in the room empty except for these brown repositories of her memories of Michigan. She knew that as she opened them, their contents unfolding and spreading across the floors and up the walls, it would be the unfolding of her imagination, only more satisfying. The driver of the truck kept telling her how lucky she was to be living in Florida. He was a big black man with a toothpick in his mouth and a long black comb in his back pocket.

"Love this weather down here," he said, resting for a moment on the handles of his hand truck as he paused in the doorway and gazed into the mottled yard of sun and shade. "Love these one-month winters."

He told her he'd lived in Ocala with his sister one year and how in late January he'd been surprised when she started talking about getting ready for their Welcome to Spring party. "I thought she was off it and I told her," he said. "Gettin' up for a party two months away." He laughed and rocked on the hand truck. "Come to find out, down here spring don't wait that long. She was talking about next week." He leaned the hand truck back on its wheels, pushing it back and forth and sideways as if he were dancing with it.

When the movers left and she was alone in the house, she felt glad that she, and not Pete, had been there to direct them and organize everything. She was responsible now, not him. So far, everything in the move had been his, the new job, the plans, the trip down to find the house. Now, it was becoming hers. She went to the kitchen to fix some tea on the stove. Gas, she hadn't used a gas stove for years, not since she stayed with her grandmother in the summers when she was a girl. That faint, sweet smell as she turned the knob, before the pilot lighted the burner. She would go into the kitchen and the little dog her grandmother kept would follow her, its small black eyes looking up at her expectantly. Puffy, that was the dog's name. She had tried to remember the name before. It had come back to her. Puffy, with her squeaky bark that sounded like a rubber heel scraping linoleum.

Something made her look up from the stove. There was a face at the window. A woman's face. She was there for a moment, and then she was moving toward the back door.

A tap on the glass. Janice turned down the flame under the kettle.

When she opened the door, a woman in her late-fifties was on the stoop, leaning forward as if she were straining to see through the screen and past Janice into the recesses of the house.

She peered up into Janice's eyes and smiled. The lips of her small, round mouth were heavy with red lipstick. She was wearing an old gray sweater that bagged out in the front and on the sides above the waist. "I'm Eveline," she said, her Southern accent thick, rising on the last syllable. "I came over to see if you needed any help. Being that the movers have gone and you're here alone."

"I'm Janice." She opened the door. "I don't need any help, but you're welcome to come in. I was just making tea."

Eveline, who in spite of the bulk of her sweater was actually very thin, glided past her and into the kitchen.

"I used to practically live here with the last people," she said. "They were my best friends." She paused and then, absently, said, "The Rodgers." Walking to the edge of the living room, she looked at the furniture and boxes. "You'll be needing some help," she said.

When the tea was ready, they sat at the table and drank it slowly, neither of them saying much. From her first impression, Janice had

expected the woman to be a talker, but Eveline seemed more intent on gazing around the room, drinking her tea in little sips.

After she finished, she said, "When it's empty like this I can
almost see it the way it was, you know." She looked at Janice and
her quick eyes wrinkled at the corners.

"You mean when the Rodgers lived here?" Janice said.

"Oh no. Of course, I can still remember that. I mean when I
used to live here with Sam and the boys." She didn't stop, and her
voice ran on, light and crisp, so that Janice thought of a brook, the
ice melting, the air still so cold that the water ran in tiny shatter-
ings of ice over the pebbles. "He worked at the Springs," she said.
"Ran one of the boats. The water's like glass, you know. You can
see all the way down." Then she paused. "You haven't been, have
you?" she said. "I can tell by looking at you."

Janice shook her head. She had heard of the Springs, but of
course she hadn't been. There were so many things to do. It wasn't
the kind of thing she liked anyway. Feeling like a tourist made the
skin on her arms itch.

"We'll go," Eveline said. "We'll go next week after I help you
get moved in."

Before Janice could say anything, before she could put down
the foot that she sensed would need to be put down, Eveline had
stood up and walked to the hallway, motioning with her arm for
Janice to follow.

"Now we'll have to have a talk about the boys' room," she said.
The arm swooped more insistently. Janice rose from the table and
followed.

Later that day, after Eveline had left, Janice was sitting again
at the table, waiting for Pete to come home. The light was getting
dim when she heard the car come up the drive. She went to the

door to meet him. On the steps he looked gray and stooped, older she thought. He was always doing that, changing himself when he didn't know she was watching him. How easily he could change into an old man, as if their life together were a distant memory. Seeing him that way hurt her. Those were the times she felt his sadness at their not having children the worst, when guilt rose up inside her and she wished she had given in to him.

She'd been waiting for hours to tell him about the woman, but when she saw him the words sank back into her. He opened the door, and she stood there without saying anything.

"Hey, babe," he said, his face bright and young again.

She stepped back and let him into the room. "Dinner's not ready yet," she said.

What she had wanted to tell him was that their new neighbor was completely nuts. She wanted to watch his reaction when she described the way Eveline started dancing when she entered the room with the painted figures. It was "the boys' room." She never called them by their names.

Then Janice would have taken him down the hall and shown him the figures on the wall again, made him look at them closely. He would have seen that they were not painted on the top layer of paint but were surrounded by layer after layer, until they appeared sunken in the wall.

He would have said something like "So?" And he would have looked at her blankly.

Then she would have explained how Eveline had come each time over the years when new people had moved in.

Sitting at the table before Pete returned home, Janice had pictured how she would tell him. He wouldn't understand at first. He would shrug his shoulders.

"Don't you get it?" she would say.

"Get what?"

"She won't let anybody paint over them."

"Oh," he would say.

Then she would let him have it. "Because they're dead," she would say. "Her boys who lived in the room are dead."

But she'd seen him on the stoop and then had told him nothing. It's too creepy anyway, she thought later that night. They were lying side by side on the floor in their sleeping bags, and she looked over at him. The yellow porch light came in through the window on the side of his face. Outside, it had started to rain and the drops running down the glass made moving shadows on his nose and cheek.

"Why did you move out?" she had asked Eveline.

"Move out?" she'd said. "Oh no. We moved back. We moved back into the neighborhood." Then she paused for a moment and said softly, "My Sam didn't much like the idea though." She took a small, folded handkerchief from a pocket in her blouse and rubbed a place on one of the paintings. Janice noticed for the first time how much older and darker the paint was. The whites were dingy, as if there had been a smoker in the room. There was nothing a handkerchief could do, but Eveline went around, touching a spot here and there, sometimes rubbing the paint for a few moments.

"I might need to paint the room," Janice said, "to make it brighter." She hadn't thought of doing any such thing until just then. It was creepy the way Eveline was touching the walls. It made Janice feel as if she herself were being worked over. "I might paint it yellow," she said, even though she hated yellow.

Eveline only continued rubbing gently at the animals with her hanky. There was a sweet smile on her face and she hummed softly, a song Janice couldn't make out.

That night as she lay awake next to Pete on the living-room

floor and listened while his breathing became slower and deeper, Janice felt a chill coming into her. The boys, two dead boys without names, and their room back down the hall, just over her husband's rising and falling chest, like a grave that woman was tending.

Janice rose from the sleeping bag and went quietly to the end of the hall, opening the door and entering the room. In the dim light through the windows the animals no longer seemed as lively and colorful as they did in the day. They swam around her like the ghosts of a life over which she had no control. She shuddered and went back to the living room and stared down at Pete, who was curled on his side. His breath moved the sheet, making the shadows in its folds swell and bend like the stripes on a tiger. Should she have stayed single? Sometimes she liked having another person to keep her from doing everything just as she always had, and sometimes it was unbearable.

She lay down beside him and curled against his back. The warm smell of his skin comforted her. She fell asleep.

The next day she began to unpack boxes and fill the living room with their familiar things. She wanted to do it slowly, to savor it. Unwrapping the paper, she made a game of pretending she didn't know what was inside. She imagined strange things, like dried creatures from a museum, and precious things, like jeweled goblets and delicate crystal. Taking off the wrappings was like expecting an ogre or the queen of England to come to your door. It was exciting and horrible at the same time. Then she'd open the door to find a comfortable old friend instead.

In the middle of the afternoon, Eveline returned, with an apple pie she'd just baked. She didn't stay, but Janice could see that the woman intended to make her coming over a regular affair. It was spooky, as if Eveline were visiting her past and Janice were an interloper, as if Janice herself were the ghost and the boys were real.

When Pete came home, she fixed them a spaghetti dinner and afterwards they sat in the living room and hooked up the wires for the stereo so they could have music. Pete wanted to put up the bed, but Janice didn't let him. She wanted to camp out in the living room one more night. They made love wildly across the floor.

In the middle of the night she awoke. She had the feeling that someone was outside, trying to see in around the curtains. Janice felt as if the house were surrounded. As if a hundred Evelines were trying to see in.

She sat up and looked over at Pete. He was on his back and his face was as pale as the belly of a fish. It scared her. She started to put her head to his chest to see if he was still breathing, but then he shifted and rolled onto his stomach. Janet got up and went to the kitchen.

Under the sink were two cans of white paint and some brushes the landlord had left for them in case they wanted to repaint the walls. She took one of the cans and the brushes, closing the cabinet door carefully.

The boys' room was darker than the living room but there was enough light from the two windows, which still didn't have curtains. She didn't want to turn on the light. Through the side window she saw Eveline's house. The porch light was on, but the rest of the house was dark. The rain dripped from the pines and from the Spanish moss that hung from the big live oak between their two houses.

She used a butter knife from the kitchen to open the can, and she dipped in the brush. She realized that she should spread down papers to catch the drips, but there was no time for that. The work went quickly. She didn't try to paint all of the walls, just the parts where the animals were, and around them to feather the paint. She went back over the depressions again and again with more coats of paint.

There was a noise behind her and she froze.

"What are . . . doing?" Pete said. She turned and saw him wavering in the doorway, rubbing his eyes.

"What does it look like I'm doing?"

"Can't . . . wait till tomorrow? I could hear you slapping that." His voice slurred. "In the bedroom . . . room."

"Go back to sleep. I can't explain it. I just have to do it now."

He didn't say anything and looked around. Then he wandered into the bathroom. The door closed and opened a moment later. His foot scuffed the carpet down the hall. There was a soft thump as he dropped back onto the sleeping bag.

The room with its newly blank walls seemed very empty. She put the top back on the paint can and went into the bathroom, turning on the light and washing the brush in the sink. The white paint swirled in the water like milk. When she finished cleaning up, she didn't look into the room again.

That's the end of that, she said to herself as she walked down the hall to the living room. She stretched out on her back on the sleeping bag and put her hands under her head. The rain dripping from the eaves made a steady tapping on the cement steps. She imagined she was in a tent in the woods.

The next day, Eveline did not appear as Janice had expected. No face peering in the kitchen window, no tap at the door. Janice had dreaded the confrontation, but when Eveline didn't appear it bothered her even more. Her one pride was taking care of things like that quickly.

For the next several days, Janice was busy unpacking boxes.

Each time she filled a room, it reminded her of one of those sponges that is nothing but a little ball until you put it in water and the legs and neck and head of an animal start to pop out. By early the next week she had finished her unpacking and was ready to get back to her writing.

She decided to stick with her original intention to make the boys' room her writing room. *The boys' room,* she hated herself when she thought of it that way, but she couldn't stop. Her writing table was by the window on the side of the house. She had not wanted to face Eveline's, but on the other hand the big oak with its drooping moss enchanted her. She could look at it for hours and get lost in its gnarled branches and the way the gray moss curled down like tangled hair.

To her left on the wall was the picture of the singing alligator, the only one that the paint had not completely covered. She couldn't always see it, but when the light was just right, there it would be, holding out its stubby arms and singing to her.

She was working on a story she'd started in Ann Arbor about a character named Ed. She wasn't sure yet who or what Ed would turn out to be, and maybe that was the way it should be for the reader of the story. A mystery about the children in a family who were in love with Ed, but wouldn't tell who he was. Every time the parents would ask them if they wanted anything, all they would say was, "Ed instead!"

"Do you want ice cream for dessert?"

"Ed instead!"

"How would you like to go to the beach today?"

"Ed instead!"

By midweek she was almost to the end of the story, and she still didn't know what Ed was going to be. In the story the parents had become frantic wanting the children to tell them who or what Ed was. And she was just as frantic herself. She'd been staring at the oak tree for at least an hour but nothing had come to her. After a slow drizzle all morning, the clouds were breaking up and the sun was coming in through the back window. Suddenly, beside her, the alligator was holding out its arms. She looked at it. Its stupid awkward mouth was calling her.

"Forget it, buster!" she said. "I got rid of your pals. Just because you're still around. . . ." In the corner of her eye, she caught sight of Eveline crossing the yard between their houses. "Uh-oh," she said to the alligator.

She didn't hear a tap at the kitchen door, but she went anyway. Eveline was on the stoop. She was holding a basket in her right hand, and when Janice opened the door, she held it up.

"Picnic day!" she said. The thick red lipstick spread into a big smile. She shook the basket in the doorway. "I promised you a trip to the Springs. And I'm not one to go back on my word."

Confronted by the shaking basket, Janice took a step backward. "I'm sorry," she said. "I can't. Not today. I'm working."

"Now, now," Eveline said. "I've been sick all week long and I didn't help you a lick with getting settled." In an instant, she had eased through the doorway and past Janice. "Oh my," she said looking around the kitchen and into the living room, "it's wonderful in here. You didn't need me at all."

"Thank you," Janice said. "Listen, I'm sorry you went to the trouble to make a lunch. I have to work this afternoon, and I can't. . . ."

"Work!" Eveline said. "After all this rain, and this is the first sunny afternoon in a week? My, my, honey. This is the first touch of spring we've had. You're lucky I came over."

She took Janice by the hand. "Just do an old lady a favor," she said. "You'll thank me later." She winked and gave Janice's hand a couple of little tugs toward the door. Janice didn't want to go, but guilt over painting the walls surged up unexpectedly and broke down her resolve. Maybe out of the house, confessing to painting over the animals would be easier. She would go along, be neighborly, and then her most venomous realm of conscience would have to tone down its whisper that she'd painted over the old bat's memories out of spite.

Eveline's car, an ancient Plymouth with big fins, had pine needles stuck by sap across its hood, and they whipped in the wind like long stiff fur while the car swayed down the highway south of town, past the old gas stations, the run-down stores, the yards with weathered signs in them advertising mullet and shrimp and crabs. Janice felt she'd sunk into someone's stereotype of the South. It came up around her in the musty smell of the Plymouth with its spots of mildew on the seats and dash. No one seemed to throw anything away. In the yards were rotting boats, piles of rusted metal. She saw a line of plaster ducks deep in grass, half of them toppled over, a drunken migration turned to stone.

Eveline started singing.

You get a line, and I'll get a pole,
And we'll go fishing in the crawdad hole.
Baby, baby, won't you be mine?

Janice smiled. It was something her mother had sung to her when she was little. She put her arm out the window, and the cool air made the hair stand up on her skin. Maybe this was what she needed, to get away from that infernal house. And maybe a friend wasn't a bad thing either, if they could just get past that craziness of the painted room. As Eveline began the next verse, Janet started singing along. Soon they were coming into the park, and she saw the main lodge house and the parking lot, which was almost empty except for a couple of buses.

"They don't run the boats much this time of year," Eveline said. "But I called and there's a church school group here today from Bainbridge. That's up in Georgia."

Once out of the car, Eveline steered Janice to a picnic table near the dock and they sat down. The main pool of the Springs was a couple of hundred feet across, with a beach area on their side and on the other a thick jungle of vegetation. About thirty feet out from the beach was a big white and blue diving platform. No one was swimming, but on the dock for the tour boats a crowd of children was chattering and squealing.

"I haven't been here in years," Eveline said, "not since Sammy passed on." She put the picnic basket on the table and lifted the top. "We can have a little something now," she said, "if you want."

"Do we need tickets for the boat?" Janice said.

"Oh no. I fixed that with Mr. Jenson. He runs the place." She pulled out a thermos and a couple of plastic cups from the basket. Janice thought it was very quaint how she'd made pink lemonade, a summer drink. She could imagine how the Springs would be in the warm weather. Kids everywhere, diving into the water, floating on their inner tubes, screaming and running along the shore.

"Listen," she said. "I've got something to tell you." She looked at Eveline, who was watching the children on the dock as she sipped her lemonade.

Eveline put her cup down and turned to Janice. "You sound so serious," she said. "It must be about the pictures in the boys' room." Before Janice had time to answer, she went on. "I know what you did. I knew you would the minute I heard your voice."

Janice looked at her, puzzled.

"I knew you had to control things," continued Eveline. "You're just like me."

"Now wait a minute." Janice felt angry. Then guilty. It was too complicated for her to understand.

A horn tooted. "The boat's leaving," Eveline said. "We'd better hurry." She closed the picnic basket and stood up.

Janice didn't want to go on the boat anymore, but Eveline was already heading down the path to the dock. Things couldn't be left hanging this way. She got up from the table and followed.

The front half of the boat was already full of kids. Janice stepped down from the dock into the swaying boat and started to sit on the wooden bench beside Eveline.

"Wait," said Eveline, "You should sit on the outside so you can see down in the water." She got up and nudged Janice past her.

Janice glanced over the side. Several feet down, the long grasses were swept by the current. A school of large fish swam past.

"Those are mullet," Eveline said. She was right next to Janice's ear, leaning beside her as if she were whispering secrets. "They swim up from the Gulf of Mexico and get big and fat and sassy in here. They know they're safe inside the park."

The motor started and the guide, a man in his forties with a balding head of red hair and heavy freckles, had already begun his pitch. "Now here on your left, you will be approaching the dreaded island of the gators. Some of these monsters are over two hundred years old." He looked back at the children. "That's even older than your mommas and daddies." No one laughed, but one child screamed and pointed toward an alligator that turned out to be a log. Then they saw a real alligator. It lay motionless on the bank, soaking up the noonday sun.

"I didn't tell you my boys drowned, did I?" said Eveline. Her voice was distant. At first, Janice thought she sounded nostalgic, but that wasn't it. Not sad either.

Damn, Janice thought, can't we just drop this? She'd wanted to clean up the matter of the paintings, and now they were even deeper into it. The boys. Dead boys. You could never just talk that away. She shook her head in answer to Eveline's question.

"We were down at the coast, a place on St. George Island we used to visit with our church group on Sunday afternoons."

Janice watched the passing shoreline, the cage with the trapped black bear pacing back and forth, the anhinga bird sitting on a limb and spreading its wings to dry. The guide was rattling on about these things while Eveline told about the death of her boys. Their names were Randy and Jeff. Jeff, the younger one, had been drawn down by the undertow. Randy had drowned, too, trying to save him.

Janice could see nothing of the lodge anymore, only the hanging jungle-like vegetation, with alligators lying along the bank, and dozens of cranes and anhingas. The clear water rushed under the boat like a thick wind full of schools of fish. She was half listening to Eveline and half to the enthusiastic guide, the tragedy of the boys drowning mixed up with the thrill of imagining how it would be to travel through a jungle and lose your way.

The boat circled around an island and through a long pass like a leafy cave between overhanging trees as the guide chattered on about the Tarzan movies filmed there during the 1930s. "Look," Eveline said, "we're back at the main spring." The boat swung out of the narrow channel behind the island and into the deeper water of the big pool. Janice looked down, but she couldn't see the bottom anymore. The guide stopped the boat.

"Now this here is the haunt of the world's most famous bass," he said. "The mighty Henry, reputed to weigh near twenty pounds." He took out a walking cane and held it over the side of the boat, parallel to the water's surface and about two feet above it. Then he tapped his knuckles on the side of the boat. "Come on now, Henry," he said. "Let's show these fine boys and girls what you can do."

Eveline was beside herself with excitement. "You won't believe this," she said. "Sammy used to do this. It comes right out of the water and jumps over the pole."

"A trained fish?" Janice said. She was astonished. How could you train a wild fish?

"Come on now, Henry," the man was saying. He rapped his knuckles again. The cane stuck out over the water, and its shadow hovered beneath the surface like a dark board waving into the depths. The children were leaning over the side, trying to see the miraculous fish as it came up. "Come on now, Henry," the man said. "It's springtime." He waved the cane a little and rapped his knuckles harder.

"Come on now, Henry," one little voice squeaked.

Then another. "Come on now, Henry."

The rest of the children giggled.

Then they were all saying it, Eveline and Janice and even the two prim Baptist women who'd brought the children on their trip.

"Come on now, Henry."

"Come on now, Henry." Until Janice and Eveline and the children were looking at one another and laughing, no longer staring down into the water, or even at the man, who by then had realized how foolish he was, holding the cane over the water.

The children were still tittering when Janice turned to Eveline.

"I'm sorry," she said. "I'm sorry about your boys, I mean. But the house is mine now and I had to paint over the pictures." She expected Eveline to look sad or angry, but she didn't. She was smiling. Janice wondered if the woman was unbalanced. "Don't you think it hurts you to keep remembering?" she said.

Eveline nodded. "After I saw you through the window, in the middle of the night, painting over those pictures, I had a dream about bringing you here," she said. "I was so mad I threw you in the water so you'd see how it felt. But we were both in the water and we tried to save each other. We just kept going down and down."

Janice tightened her grip on the railing. She was trying to read Eveline's face, but she couldn't.

"When we let go of each other, we floated up." Eveline patted Janice on the knee. "It's horrible when you have to protect something, and you can't."

Janice didn't know what to say.

"You're just like me," Eveline said. "We can't help it when we're desperate."

Janice thought about the night when she painted over the pictures. Was it desperation? It was, although she wouldn't have described it that way at the time. But why? She remembered the way her heart sank when Pete drove them into the yard and she saw the house. She'd hated it. Yet, when Eveline tried to insinuate her way into it, she, Janice, had latched onto it as fiercely as if her own dead children had lived there.

The man with the cane sighed and put it back under his seat. He shook his head. "Must be the cold. He must be sleeping down deep on a day like this," he said.

Just before he restarted the boat, Janice looked into the water and saw a shadow hovering. She couldn't tell what it was, but she wanted to say it was the elusive Henry. Maybe it was watching them, just a heartbeat away from leaping out of the water, for whatever purpose.

The Ocean

Stop killing your father. Go to the ocean. Love a woman. When you're young, things are supposed to be that simple.

The last morning in San Antonio behind the motel-office window, for me the only simple things are the cool air and the quiet while I watch the sun rise in the field of junked cars behind the parking lot. At five-thirty I go out to check the ice machine. In the hot, dry air of the hallway I open the box and find pale yellow water shuddering in the bottom. I shovel it out with a square ice bucket and tape the out-of-order sign to the lid. The sun hangs between the stacks of flattened bodies by the fence like a big dull torch. Later, when it's high and too bright to look at, I'll hate it. But now the sun is down between the rows of flattened cars. I feel like walking out to it. Everything around us is simple and quiet.

The morning will still be quiet for a while. Then the orange doors will open and people will come out of their rooms to load their trunks. The cars roar and the parking lot begins to empty. Before it empties all the way, it starts to fill again. It reminds me of the ocean. I've never seen the ocean, but I've heard about it.

Amy told me. Amy, who's the twenty-five-year-old divorcée who works mornings cleaning out the rooms. We were in one of the rooms together and we were rolling on the bed. Nothing serious, just to have fun, Amy said, because he was too young for her, she said. She always used *he* when she talked about me and sex.

"I'm sixteen," I said. "I'm old enough to quit school."

She laughed and hit me over the head with a pillow.

"Maybe you are, but he's not," she said.

Then we were lying on our backs, and she was talking about the ocean.

"You ain't been to the ocean, have you?" she said. She had her elbows up in the air and her hands behind her head so they puffed out her wavy brown hair. From the side, her short thick nose was like the one on a doll my two little sisters had. But her body was lean and hard. Sometimes when we were rolling around she would wrap her arms around me and squeeze me until I couldn't breathe.

"No, I haven't been," I said. "I told you I'd never been fifty miles out of San Antonio." I didn't want to talk. I was hurt because she'd stopped me again when I tried to pull up her dress.

"You can just lie on your back at the edge of it, and it comes in and goes out, up and down, that warm water all over you."

"I don't want to hear about it," I said.

"When it runs out past you, it sucks the sand around you. You feel like you're going to be sucked right down under the sand if you lie there long enough."

"I said I don't want to hear."

"It's like heaven."

I rolled away from her and said I never wanted to see her again.

She laughed and bit my ear so hard it started to bleed.

Usually, it's the older tourists from up north who come out of their rooms first. I can make a good guess of the time of day by the tags left in the lot. Michigan, Minnesota, New York. It's still early.

Later they're gone and Oklahoma, Kansas, Missouri are left. The people come out of their rooms and look up toward the sun, not right at it, just in the direction of it, and then they look down at the pavement and shake their heads. The last to go are from Texas. Texas people have a way with the sun.

On the counter in front of me in the office is the jar where my father, Ernesto, keeps the scorpion. Ernesto is the only father I've got, and I hate him. He is an uneducated man and likes it that way. He says I never had a real father. He tells everyone he found me in a laundry cart at the motel and that was my father, my mother, too. José, who comes twice a week to clean the pool, found the scorpion trapped in the trough around the edge of the pool. It was a kind no one had ever seen around here, black and evil looking. Ernesto put it in a jar and told everybody he found it hiding under the sheets of a bed. He teases Amy with it. My father is a fat man who is like the joke of a father. He has a silver tooth in the front of his mouth. He smiles his wet smile and says that my last name is Industra-Klean, after the name of the laundry cart. Juan Industra-Klean, it has a nice sound to it, no? Ernesto is the biggest jerk in the world.

"Look Amy, what I want to give you," he will say when she comes in to turn in the room keys. He waves the jar with the scorpion in it and leers at her.

Ernesto only comes in after lunch, hardly ever in the mornings. He likes to come in when the maids get through so he can try to get them to go somewhere with him for the afternoon. When he has left with one of them, usually the small ugly one named Manuela, I kill him. So far I have done it sixteen times, mostly with the scorpion, mostly by pressing his fat hand down onto its tail. I have seen a movie where two cowboys in Mexico tie two scorpions to a table and then arm wrestle over them. The loser's hand is mashed into the tail. But in the movie the loser cheats. He grabs a bottle and breaks it. He stabs the bite and sucks out the poison. I keep thinking the cheater is John Wayne, but maybe it isn't, because John Wayne never did any *pendejo* shit like that. I make sure there are no bottles Ernesto can reach when I kill him.

One morning the week after I told Amy I never wanted to see her again, we were lying on a bed until we forgot the time. She was telling me how much she wanted a dog, a brown one with a white spot on its face, when Ernesto drove up. We heard his horn, the five notes of "Shave and a Haircut" that he always blows to let everyone know the king is in his court. My friends tell me that across the border playing those notes means *chinga tu madre,* and a man will shoot you for it. In this great country Ernesto can get by with anything.

"We'd better go," I said.

"I want him to find us," Amy said. She sat up and looked across the lot. Ernesto was getting out of his car and swinging his weight like a big sack of rocks as he closed the door of the Continental. She waved at him.

"Why did you do that?" I said.

"I want him to know I don't give a crap what he thinks."

"I know what he'd think. He'd fire us." I was thinking about my mother. She'd beat my *culito* if I lost the job. She took most of what I made as soon as I got it. Then she'd call Ernesto a silver-toothed pig. They hadn't seen each other in years. She'd always tried to keep me away from him until he called about the job two summers ago. She said I needed to learn what he was like, as if I didn't already know. She laughed at the idea that he'd be paying me to find out what a *cabrón* he was.

Amy smiled and ran her hand through my hair. "You've got beautiful hair, Juan," she said. "Long and dark and thick. I'd kill for hair like yours." She took her hand away and ran it through her own hair. She stopped for a second. Her fingers were still hanging near her head, like the hand of a dancer stopped in midstep.

"You don't think he'd fire us?" I said.

"What?" she looked at me like she'd been somewhere else. She jumped up from the bed and straightened the spread. Her palms and fingers flattened and slid across it like two irons. "You don't know him," she said. "There's nothing he'd like better than to find us. He'd think it proved I was cheap. Nothing turns him on more than thinking of himself as a big fat man owning a cheap woman."

I killed him that afternoon for the fifteenth and sixteenth times. He'd left with Tina, the new girl, who was just a year older than me. Tina was a runaway and she was only planning to stay for a few weeks. Why go with him? Why, when she was going to leave anyway? So I killed him twice that afternoon, once with the scorpion and once by shoving his face down into the ice bin until his head turned blue.

That was why I asked for the night shift. It was scaring me how many times I was having to kill him. It would only get worse. One scorpion wouldn't be enough, I'd need several, a whole army of scorpions, a car full, Ernesto's Continental full of scorpions and him trapped inside, his fat helpless face pressed against the glass of the side window while scorpions penetrated his shaking flesh.

In the office on the early morning shift the low, cool silence of the sun comes through the window and drains the hate from me. Ernesto does not exist in the morning. I wait for Amy. Her blue Volkswagen Beetle will putt past the window to the back of the lot. She'll park by the fence where the junked cars are piled. She'll get out, and I'll watch her stand by her car and brush her hair,

slip the brush into her purse, and then turn toward me, walking
to the office.

Amy, I'll say when she comes through the door, why are we
here? Why don't we get out of here? And she'll say, I've always
wanted that, Juan. I've always wanted you. . . . By that time we're
hugging, and we walk out the door, across the parking lot toward
the piles of junked cars, toward her car, the blue Volkswagen,
parked on the edge. You're the man I would never let myself have,
she says. I was lying when I told you about going to the bars at
night with other men. I didn't want you to fall in love with me because I loved you, and I knew you were too good for me.

We get into the car, and then we're out of the parking lot, on
the highway, and the wind rushes through the windows of the
blue Volkswagen and around my arms and through Amy's brown
hair. Her eyes tighten into a smile, south, we're heading south for
Laredo.

I stop killing my father.

The buzzer over the front door goes off, and a short man carrying a tiny white dog on his left arm comes into the office. "Hey,
bud," he says, "got any ice in here?"

I shake my head and tell him I'm sorry about the ice machine.

"Cripes," the man says out of the corner of his mouth, like he
usually has a cigar there and likes to spit his words around it. The
dog, who has on a pink collar with gold letters spelling LULU, begins to squirm. It's so small its little head looks like a golf ball he's
squeezing in the crease of his elbow.

"There's a quick mart down the road," I say, pointing out the
window in the direction past the junked cars.

The man stares at the scorpion in the jar. He moves closer until
his nose is right against the glass. The dog begins to whine.

"It's deadly, ain't it?" he says.

"Not really. I don't know, for sure," I say. He doesn't believe me. The look in his eyes reminds me of Ernesto when he stares at Amy.

"How much?" he says.

"How much?"

"For the bug, the. . . ."

"Scorpion?"

"Yeah. How much you want for it?"

"It's not for sale."

"Cripes, boy. It's just a bug. How much is it?"

"It's not mine."

"Then whose is it?" He pushes the dog's face up to the glass, and the way the dog is squirming I know it will knock over the jar.

"It belongs to Mr. Ernesto, he's the manager. But he's not here," I say.

"Then who's going to know?"

His puffy cheeks are red and oily. Except for his eyes, he's a happy elf. I've seen ones like him, the tourists hovering around the Alamo, the proud defenders. They carry knives between their teeth. They dream of themselves behind the wall. Their sharp little eyes watch Santa Anna's army prepare to swarm over them like brown wasps. They like it.

When I don't say anything, he takes the dog's nose away from the jar. "One hundred dollars," he says.

"I can't."

"We'll say the dog knocked it over."

I think about the hundred dollars. I think about me and Amy in her car, rushing down the highway. We aren't going to Laredo, we're going to the ocean. I feel myself lying on my back in the sand the way she has told me. The water rushes around my body, me and Amy, the two of us together. We hold hands and feel the water suck us down together.

Stop killing your father. Go to the ocean.

He slaps his palm flat on the counter. Under it is a hundred-dollar bill. "I don't even want to keep the bug," he says. "I just want to borrow it for five minutes. It's just to play a joke."

He smiles. He's not telling the truth, but what difference does it make? It's Ernesto's scorpion, and I hate Ernesto. I hate it when he teases Amy with the scorpion, and I hate myself when I think of killing him with the scorpion. The scorpion. Damn the scorpion. I reach for the hundred-dollar bill, and the man's hand slides slowly away from the top of it.

Ernesto is not my father. I'll go to the ocean.

"Good," the man says. "Now I need someplace I can go. Someplace I can be alone."

I look into the face of the hundred-dollar bill. I think about Amy. She will drive into the lot at any minute. I'll tell her, we can go away together.

"Hey, Jack," the man says.

I remember what he asked. "Back there," I say, pointing to the room where the linens are kept. He picks up the jar and takes it and the dog into the back. From the highway comes the sound of Amy's car. I recognize the way she downshifts the gears, and the little car revs up like it's about to explode before it screeches into the entrance of the parking lot. I look out the window, and my heart jumps as I see her, her flock of hair wild and free. Amy, I say inside. Amy, I've got to tell you.

I love a woman.

There's a piercing yelp from the back room and the crash of glass on the floor. I jump over the counter, but before I reach the doorway, the man hurries out with the dog, pulling it on its leash and choking it as it whines and struggles to get away. The dog tries to dig its claws into the carpet, but he jerks it across the lobby in a series of short hops like a white frog.

"Sorry as hell about the glass," he says. "Here's something for your trouble." He throws another hundred-dollar bill at me. Before I can say anything, he is out the door and the bill is drifting behind him from side to side as it drops to the floor.

At the window I watch him drag the dog back to their room. Near the door he starts to yell, "Honey, honey!" The dog's back legs have swung sideways so that it's being dragged across the pavement. "A terrible thing has happened!" he yells.

An enormous woman in a red dress, so large she reaches both sides of the doorway, spills into the opening and through it. The dog is completely down on its side and the woman looks at it with her mouth open and puffing. She tries to bend down to it, but she's too big.

Across the lot Amy watches by her car while the woman yells at the man. I can't make out any words. The woman's mouth forms a large O, and the sounds that come from it are like screeching metal, like in the pit of her an old car is being crushed flat.

I go to the ocean. The water comes up around my body.

I open the door. I hear the man. "It was an accident, honey . . . by the ice machine . . . some kind of a bug."

The woman tries with her huge arms to scoop up the dog but she can't reach it. The dog's tongue is out on the pavement. Its eyes are closed and its body is still.

Then Amy, who has been standing by her car the whole time, rushes over and grabs the dog. The head rolls over her forearm, and the tongue lolls out. She holds the body close to the woman, but the woman doesn't look at it. Her thick hands fly out to the man's neck, and she begins to choke him, shaking him like a fence post she's trying to loosen from its hole.

"You murdering bastard," she screams. "You'll never get another piece out of me." She drops him and goes to a metallic blue van, jerks open the door, and climbs into the driver's seat. She cranks the motor and screeches into reverse, past the man and Amy, then jams it into forward and roars past the office onto the highway.

The man darts his eyes at Amy and the dog, then at the open door of his room. He doesn't seem to know what to do. He sees me standing by the office and waves me over.

"Listen," he says, shouting across the lot. "We've had a little trouble here. There's been a little misunderstanding."

I take a few steps. Amy is confused, holding the dog in her arms, and I want to go to her. But I don't want to have anything else to do with the man.

"I'm going to need a cab," he shouts.

"Get it yourself," I say.

"What's that?"

"There's a phone in the office."

He rushes past me and into the office. Standing outside the room, Amy is stiff and holds the dog like they are trapped with no idea of which way is out. The sun's heat rising from the asphalt is so strong that the hot air presses against me like a thick, dry blanket.

"I think it's dead," she says when I get to her.

Its eyes aren't completely closed. I can see about half of the pupils, filmy and brown. "Can you feel its heart?" I say.

She tries to feel with her fingers, but she can't tell.

"Let's take it in the office, Juan," she says. "Let's see what he wants to do with it."

When we take the dog in, the man is finishing on the phone.

"I'm all set," he says. "Cab will be here in a few minutes."

"Should we take Lulu to your room?" I say.

"Lulu?"

"The dog."

"Cripes," the man says. "What would I do with it?"

"I don't know," I say.

"Look, boy, I don't have time now. Maybe you can take care of it. Here's another fifty," he says. He reaches into his pocket and tries to stuff a bill into my hand.

"No." I jerk my hand away.

"Fine," the man says. "See you later, kid. Enjoy the dog." We watch him cross the lot and go into his room. Behind the open door he is throwing clothes into a suitcase on the bed.

Amy puts the dog on the couch in the office and sits down beside it, smoothing its fur. She is quiet for a minute and then she says, "What did he mean, another fifty?"

Her hair is messed up the way I love it, and her blue eyes wait for me. I can't lie to her. My legs go weak. I sit on the floor.

"I thought we could go away," I say. "I thought we could just get the hell out of here." Little black suns are spinning in a yellow sky.

"What are you talking about?" she says.

"I didn't know what he was going to do."

I look up and see that she's not mad at me. "That's why I took it," I say.

"You're not making any sense, Juan."

I'm crying, with my legs out in front of me, crying like a little kid. I've broken something, and I don't understand. How do things break anyway? They shouldn't break.

Then I think of how once they're broken, they're calm. Nothing else can happen. Do the flattened cars wait for the morning sun? They don't need it.

"I just want you to love me," I say.

"Oh, Juan." Amy gets down on the floor and hugs me. "Whatever it is," she says, "it's all right."

"I didn't mean to do it," I say. I tell her what happened, what the man did.

She looks at the dog. She's been rubbing her hand over its fur the whole time, smoothing it, running her fingers around its tiny ears and under its scrawny neck.

"How could you do that?" she says. "How could you let him kill this poor little thing?"

I kill myself. I break everything. There is no ocean. Nothing else can happen.

"I didn't know. I didn't." How could I not know?

She takes her hand away from the dog. "That bastard Ernesto," she says. "This is his fault."

I can only blame myself. We swarm over the walls of the Alamo. Its sharp-eyed defenders have vanished.

Amy stands and picks the dog up from the couch. "Come on, baby," she says, "we're getting out of here."

She has the dog draped over her palm like a fat dishrag. I don't want to look at it. She goes to the door and opens it. People are coming out of their rooms and loading the trunks of cars. They have never been real people going to real places. They came from cars that appeared from nowhere in front of the office. They walked in and out of their rooms, to the ice machine, to the pool. Now they are ready to disappear again. All that's left will be the flattened, rusting bodies, piling higher until even the sun can't get above them.

I kill everyone. I go to the ocean.

The cab drives in, and the man gets into it. Amy is still holding the door open, but I can't get up. In her arms, the dog's hanging smudge of a nose points to the floor, to me. The cab moves past the office. The man in the back does not look at us. His face is straight ahead. He is made of cloth like the angel in a Christmas play. The cab disappears.

"Why did you say it was Ernesto's fault?" I say. "He didn't do anything."

Amy looks down at me. "People you hate don't have to do anything," she says. "They hurt you without even trying." She holds the door with her foot and reaches down with her free hand to take mine and pull me up. "Come on," she says, "it's getting hot and we've got a long way to go." We're out the door and crossing the lot to the Volkswagen.

I hear the five notes of "Shave and a Haircut" and turn to see Ernesto pulling in. It's amazing luck. He never comes in the morning. I have the crazy idea to run back to the office and find the scorpion and shove it in his face. Yes, I think, by god, yes!

I move quickly, the way the ocean moves, across the parking lot and through the door of the lobby. I glide over the floor. I am melting ice. In the linen closet I turn on the light and the pieces of glass from the jar shine on the linoleum. It will be impossible to find the scorpion. But there it is, on the first shelf, resting on a stack of folded sheets like a tiny black princess. She doesn't even try to hide. I take an empty ice bucket from the next shelf, and with the top I guide her in.

Running through the lobby, I knock over the lamp, leaving it behind. At the front door, though, I stop. Ernesto and Amy are together in the middle of the lot, looking down at the dog in her arms. Ernesto smiles, but not at Amy, at the dog. Its ratty little tail twitches a few times, and it licks its lips. Damn you, I think.

The ocean stops. I open the lid of the ice bucket. The scorpion makes a quick dance around the bottom.

"Traitor," I say to it. "Judas."

There is nothing left to do but walk up to Ernesto and face him.

When I reach them, I hold out the bucket and tell him it's a going-away present. He takes it, and I lift the dog from Amy's arms and hold it up in front of him. Ernesto lowers his eyebrows and asks me what I'm doing. We're leaving, you fool, me and my dog and my woman. I lead Amy to her car, and he asks me again what I'm doing. His voice grows louder. Her car starts, and he is yelling. As we pull away, he screams.

His last scream has nothing to do with the scorpion. It is a high, wild screech. I leave him behind. I must. I love a woman. I go to the ocean.

But I can't forget him in the parking lot, with the ice bucket cradled under his arm. Ernesto. My father, my joke of a father holding his scorpion. Stop me. Stop me.

Summer Girls

I fear elegance. Maybe it's from my childhood. My grand-mother Helene, for whom I was named, would take me onto her rocking chair on the wide front porch of her house in Apalachicola, and I would gaze into the black lace around her neck and up to the earrings, the gold ones with black polished stones set in them. In the sunlight glistening from the bay, the flat black stones sparkled, two dangling weights, balancing her gray hair swept into a bun.

High, arched eyebrows. Hands that even through their fine wrinkles were as slim and tight as gloves, as if the skin wasn't skin but some radiance above the muscle and bone, which rode beneath it like a Greek statue. Grandmother Helene's voice was hard glass, and yet delicate, a piece of crystal stemware with a long fragile neck. Leanie, she called me, her little Leanie with the blond hair. She said I was just like her. She read to me all the time, so that now my thoughts often sound like her stories. Sometimes I even think in Helene's voice, yet I talk plain. The words that come from my mouth are like anybody's words.

In the front yard stood two cypress trees she said were as old as Apalachicola itself. They held their short, thin needles and their tall, gently twisting trunks like well-groomed watchmen over Helene's domain. It was there, in the rocker on her porch, that she read me the story of our namesake, Helen, and of the ships that came for her.

Then she would teach me a lesson, one of the lessons she said that the Greek Helen had learned. Only the poor, she told me, can survive elegance. I didn't believe her. I saw the pictures of beautiful women whose elegant bodies sailed like ships across the pages of magazines. I heard their voices drifting in on the radio like the long strands of a willow in the breeze, and I watched them loom twenty feet tall in the darkened movie theater that was the only place cool in the Apalachicola summer. I knew what she meant by elegance, but what did she mean by surviving it? Now I know. You do it by hardship, scraping the skin to the bone so it grows back with its scars. I work eight hours a day in a long, wooden room. Its walls are painted white, and its floor is cement. As fast as my hands can move, which is faster than I can see, I take the scrubbed oysters from the tin trough on the back of the table, I pop them with the knife, sluice out the insides into the plastic pail, and toss the shells into a box at my feet. I have tried to watch my hands, to see what it is they do, but I can't anymore. They are too fast and have a way of their own. That's the elegance I have. That, and Helene's voice, which runs in me as smooth and quick as those hands.

Now, Helene is gone, and I'm the woman who lives in the house overlooking the bay. After work I sit in my rocker on the porch and watch the oyster skiffs coming in with their upturned prows knifing the water and each owner standing in the center of his boat like a king, guiding the motor. I have no younger Helen to teach about these men or about anything else. I only have a son, and he is crazy. He has a Spanish sword he says he found in a lake. It's a miracle, he says, so remarkably preserved in the clear, cold springwater, for all the centuries since its owner lost it there. He tells me he thinks it's the sword of a murdered priest. The Indians hacked him to bits with it and threw the sword in the lake, but the priest's blood preserved it. My son, whose name is Bartholomew, a name his father gave him, spends his nights stalking the boards of the porch like the decks of a galleon, slashing the hot air with his bloodthirsty sword. In the days he works on an oyster boat and is like anyone else.

With elegance, nothing at all happens to us, this is what Grandmother Helene said. The beautiful Helen was protected, from the love-crazed kidnapper Paris and from her husband, the power-mad Menelaus. She was perfect in herself. Even the goddess who gave her as a gift knew this. Helen of ivory, Helen of alabaster, Helen of air. Elegance and protection.

The other women who work with me in the oyster-canning plant only knew Helene as a woman who spoke strangely and had an opinion of herself that ruined her life. They're my friends, and so they tell me those ideas about her because they want to save me from being like her. Imagine that Helen of Troy had a daughter by Paris, and after the war somehow she was left behind and raised by the Trojan survivors. What would they tell her about her mother? If they loved her they'd show her the ruins and tell her, "Beauty caused all this. Beauty and elegance."

There's a man in my life, but he's not my husband. My husband drowned years ago. Bartholomew is all that's left of him. This new man is named David, and he is gentle and sane.

On bright Sundays like today I sit on the porch of Helene's house and watch him and Bartholomew sailing in the bay. David has a little boat, just big enough for two or three. They usually ask me to come, but I like to sit in the rocker and watch them tacking out toward St. George and the other barrier islands. The boat has a sleek white hull and white sails with a red stripe angling down. When the boat is close I can see Bartholomew in his billowing yellow windbreaker and David with his shirt off and his browned skin like wood come alive.

Always, at some point, Bartholomew will reach into a duffel bag he carries on board and take out the Spanish sword. David handles the rudder and Bartholomew goes to the bow and stands there waving the sword and shouting. If the wind is right I can hear him, but I can't understand the words. Men are all crazy, I think. They go to war over beauty, or honor, or wealth, and when there's none of that to fight over they don't know what to do with themselves. They thrash around.

Is it necessary to be distant from everyone in order to survive? Helen of Troy must have thought so. Did she join the garden club? Was she a member of the PTA? Apalachicola is a small town on the coast. Like Troy, it has its walls and towers, but you have to live here awhile to see them. The inventor of the air conditioner lived here. Now, we live in our isolation, the windows shut. The cool air is protected.

David wants to take me away from all this. Imagine a string of Parises, each man nicer than the last, all sent by the goddess of love to take you away from all this. Some women can live that way, but I can't. I have made my stand, like Bartholomew waving his crazy sword.

Last week at the cemetery I cleaned the graves of Helene and my parents and my husband. I go there all the time. The cemetery is on a piece of high rolling ground covered with huge live oaks whose Spanish moss hangs so low it brushes your hair as you walk under the limbs. Seeing the sandy ground with the fallen moss lying on it like strands of tarnished silver filigree, I have a hard time thinking of the dead as anything more than elegant sleepers. Who would want to rise again when they could lie under the peace of those trees? There's your heart, Helene. Unmoved and unmoving. There's the heart of elegance.

As I was kneeling at the edge of Helene's grave, another woman appeared. I hadn't heard her drive up. She wandered among the stones for a while, and then she came over. She was in her early forties, dressed nicely, no one I'd ever seen before. Her forehead was high and proud.

"Hello," she said. "I don't want to bother you, but I'm looking for my father, and I can't seem to find him."

She told me the family name, Hamblin, but I hadn't heard of them.

"My father owned one of the islands offshore," she said. "We weren't from here." Her voice was thin and refined. On her fingers she had three diamond rings. I wondered what she would have been like if she'd grown up here. Would she have been beside me at the trough of oysters, her hands moving so quickly that the wet shine of the knife flashed like diamonds around her fingers?

She told me how her family used to come down from Manhattan for a month in the early spring when she was a teenager, and how one year while she was in college her mother called and said her father had come down alone and had drowned in a boating accident.

"My mother told my younger brothers and me that his body was never found," she said. Her lips formed an odd, distant smile as she looked off toward the bay. The wind brushed the blond strands of her hair in and out of the shade of the trees. I couldn't help wondering what she took pleasure in. Maybe she'd simply become accustomed to that wistful sense of a life where fathers never really die but disappear into some adventure. "We didn't find out the truth until she passed away last month," the woman said. "She told us before she died that he'd been here with another woman. My mother had him buried here because she hated him dying like that, in bed with someone else. She didn't want us to find out."

It wasn't until then that we thought to introduce ourselves. Madeline Rathson was her name. "It's the last name of my most recent husband," she said. "I've taken all their names."

I helped her look through the cemetery until finally we found the grave of her father. It was off in a corner and had a small stone. Madeline Rathson shook her head when she saw how poor it looked.

"You'd think my mother could have at least given him a better memorial," she said. She swept the hair back from her forehead. "All things considered," she added.

"Were they well off?" I said, knowing that if they owned an island they must have been. I wanted to keep her talking. I had never met anyone who reminded me so much of my Helene, that same distant graciousness. Even though she was a stranger, somehow I wanted to hold on to her.

"Oh yes," she said. "Quite."

"You shouldn't blame your mother," I said.

"No," she said.

I felt awkward. She was looking down at the grave. I wondered how I would have felt if I'd just seen my father's grave for the first time, long after the grieving had drifted away for the last time, long after the loss seemed too far in the past to ever rush on me again. Would you be more at danger then than ever? Could it overtake you with a deeper sadness when you were old and thought it was far away?

"I'll just go on and leave you here," I said.

"Oh no," she said. Her face brightened. "He's been gone a long while now," she said. "I loved him very much, but I put him to rest quite some time ago."

She seemed too sure of her feelings. "Just the same," I said, "I'd better go."

"I'm between marriages, you know," she said. "It's funny how you take the sadness of one thing and you put it into another."

"Being sad about your father caused a problem in your marriage?" I said.

"No, I mean that whenever I'm sad about losing someone I always become sad about my father. But I'm not really that sad about him, you know. Not anymore. It's just that he was my first sadness. Like there's a room where all your sadness is, and every time you go into it, well, then that first sadness always comes to greet you."

Her face was perfectly calm, the way you might imagine Helen of Troy's face, so perfectly beautiful. Surrounded by war and terrible bloodshed, and yet unable to look out her window at it with a face anything other than beautiful. It was a beauty that couldn't change, no matter how many burning towers surrounded it. "My family is over there," I said, pointing. "Would you like to see?"

"Oh yes, Leanie" she said. We took our time walking among the stones. "'Leanie,'" she said, "that's such a pretty name. What does it come from?"

I told her about my grandmother Helene and Helen of Troy. Madeline listened intently and then laughed. "She sounds like my father's mother," she said. "My mother used to say that Grandmother Hamblin was born with a golden urn in her mouth."

We both laughed, and I told her what my husband Charles said about Helene, that when she died we should have pressed her in a book. Then, I felt sad having told her. I didn't want anyone to think of Helene as some strange character.

Madeline looked at Charles's stone. "He's been gone a long time," she said.

"I've never remarried," I said. I'd often thought of Charles lying up there under the oak trees like a big root. His whole life he had been like that, like something underground that gave life to other things but had no real life of its own. Bartholomew with his sword slashing at the wind was a huge unbalanced leaf that had sprung from him without the benefit of any trunk or limb. I remembered Charles in the damp workshop where he repaired bicycles for the neighborhood children. He was a mole in the long tunnel of frames and wheels that hung from the rafters like spiny roots and thin twisted tubers. No matter how many times I saw it happen, I was always a startled to see a child rolling a bike, freshly repaired and shining with new oil, into the sunlight from the door of the shed. Then Charles, bent-shouldered, hair mussed, rubbing his hands with a greasy rag, would appear at the doorway. His face would be dark with grease and he would smile, waving the rag at the child. I felt like those children, going off into the light with my bicycle and never looking back.

"It's easier if they don't die," Madeline said.

I asked her how many times she'd been married. Three, she told me, all of them for love, although the last one had money.

"He was the one who told me I was like a body of water," she said. She smiled and dusted off a piece of the Spanish moss that had caught on her shoulder. "His name was George, and he worked in the import-export business. He said I was always changing, but I was always the same."

"He sounds like a poet," I said.

"He was a jerk. He just needed an excuse to cheat on me."

"You're very realistic," I said.

"For someone like me, you mean," she said.

"No," I said, "for anybody."

"Bodies of water are always realistic," she said, "even though they don't hold down jobs."

"I didn't mean anything by it," I said.

"People who work never trust people who don't," she said. "It's natural. You don't have to apologize for it." Her face had tightened. There was still the same beauty in it, but I'd seen that focus of light in the eyes before, in Helene and even in myself sometimes when I'd look in the mirror. There was nothing you could explain to a person when they had that light in their eyes. There was nothing you could even explain to yourself when you were the one who had it. It was the light of a person trapped in a tower they've set on fire themselves.

She took a deep breath. "I had a lover here once," she said, "out on the island one summer. I don't even remember his name now, but he was a boy from town. He worked for my father."

I didn't like the way she was looking at Charles's stone, like she was trying to remember whether it was him.

"He wasn't my first, but I was only seventeen. My father caught us out in the sand dunes one night. We never told my mother." Madeline reached up to a tree limb with both her arms and rocked against it. Her arms seemed to flow as they swung back and forth, as if the whole limb were moving with her, not firmly connected, but free, like something rocked by slow swells of water. A girlish playfulness came across her face. "My father just smiled when he saw us there naked," she said. "The boy was so scared he ran off without his clothes and never came back."

I asked her how it made her feel, her father finding her like that.

"I would have liked it better if he'd yelled at me," she said. "I can still see the look on his face. He was glad it had happened."

"Maybe he was glad somebody else was fooling around like he was," I said.

"Exactly. Only I didn't know that then. I didn't see that until my mother told me how he'd died."

I thought of summer girls like Madeline, the rich girls from up north who came down in the warm season and walked along the sidewalks of Apalachicola leaving the smell of coconut lotion mixed with soft currents of perfume. Who knows what they were like back where they came from, but here they were not real, and no one, especially the boys, seemed to care. If they carried on lives of their own back home, they'd left them behind. Helene saw me looking at a group of them once when I was ten and we'd gone to the drugstore for our weekly ice cream. The girls were five or six years older than me, and they walked so proudly in their one-piece suits that fit them like the smooth shiny surfaces of ripe plums.

"The immortals," Helene said, nodding toward them. I looked up under her wide-brimmed hat into her eyes, which fixed on the girls like the eyes of a doctor examining a suspicious mole.

I asked her what she meant. "Never mind," she said. "When you're older you'll know for yourself." I watched the girls disappear around the corner from the drugstore, the bare soles of their feet flashing as they padded up from their loose sandals.

In spite of myself, I wanted to find out more about the boy Madeline had made love with. Could it have been Charles? I knew he'd worked on the islands during the summers when he was a teenager. We'd gone steady all during high school. He told me he was a virgin. We both were.

And what of the lover in whose arms Madeline's father had died? I had a secret wish that Helene was his lover. The wish frightened me and disgusted me, but I thrilled at its possibility.

"Where do you work?" Madeline said, cutting off my thoughts.

"At the oyster-canning plant," I said.

"I noticed your hands."

"We wear gloves but it doesn't help that much. The shells still cut through sometimes." We both stared at my hands. They were red and coarse.

"I wish I'd gotten pregnant," she said.

"What?"

"I wish that boy in the dunes had made me pregnant. I wish I'd stayed here and had his baby."

"You don't even remember his name," I said.

"It doesn't matter," she said. "The important thing is this place." She turned and looked down the river toward the bay and the islands beyond it. You could just make out the line of cars along the causeway across the bay. The sun came down hard and bright on the water. "It's so far away from everything," she said. "It's so small, and it has so much around it. You can't be but one person here."

I heard the voice of Helene slipping away from me. My own voice, the voice of a woman in the oyster plant, wanted to come out. It was harsh and thick. It wanted to tell this Madeline woman she was full of crap. She was a spoiled rich girl who didn't know a damned thing about life here and had a lot of nerve trying to steal one of our men.

But what did I know? I'd never been anywhere. Helene's voice came back to me. "You could move here and see what it's like," I said.

"It wouldn't do any good. I'm too old for a family. Some man would just come and take me away."

"Who says you couldn't marry somebody from here?"

"I could," she said, "but the minute we got married he wouldn't be satisfied here anymore. Being with me would change him." She nudged her toe at the sand of Charles's grave. "I could change a dead man," she said.

Before I realized it, I swung my arm out and smacked her hard across the face with my open palm.

We were both stunned.

I looked down at my hand. Her makeup was smeared down my fingers in long streaks. She touched her cheek gently with her fingernails.

"I . . . I'm sorry," I said. "I don't know why I did that."

She sat down on the ground and started to cry. I tried to comfort her and apologize, but she wasn't listening. She was crying so loud It scared me. The big deep sobs made it hard for her to catch her breath. I ran to the car and got a box of tissues and gave her some.

She patted her face and the crying softened. "I need my mirror," she whimpered. "It's in my purse in the car." I went to her car and got the mirror for her. She dabbed her eyes with the tissues as she looked in it.

"Oh damn, oh damn!" she said. She looked up into my face. "You don't know what it's like," she said.

"What?" I said.

"Being me. Having a face you can't get away from." She shut her eyes and threw herself down violently into the sand, rubbing her face in it. Then she sat up again and took the mirror. Her skin was streaked with makeup and littered with sand and tiny bits of Spanish moss. But she was still beautiful, and although it sounds strange, she was even more elegant than she had been.

"You're so lucky you married him," she said, dabbing at her cheeks with the tissues and nodding toward Charles's grave.

I looked at the headstone, which was already becoming black-ened with spots of mildew like the oldest ones in the cemetery. I sat down beside her, and I put my arm around her shoulders, and we both cried.

Tequila Worms

$\mathbf{M}$e and Huey were on the back deck breaking out the chum when we first seen them come on board. There were five of them, a long dorky-looking kid with Coke-bottle glasses, a woman with a body like a pear and the head of a baby, two big black ones that looked like twins and were drooling down their chins, and then this old man in a captain's hat. He was the one that got to me. He wasn't goofy-looking like the rest of them. But he was blind as a tequila worm. I don't mean drunk, I mean blind like his eyes had been sucked into little wrinkly lines.

When they first come down the plank I thought they were a joke that Pud was playing on us. I just couldn't imagine him signing them on for real. I mean, my god, after all it's his boat. What happens if one of them bastards falls overboard and drowns? Can you imagine some jury getting a hold of that one? "Uh, Mr. Pud, just how long had it been since your employees scrubbed that deck to remove those dangerous oils?" God almighty.

But I went around to the cabin and peeked in and old Pud wasn't blinking an eye. He saw them coming down the plank, in lockstep, like they were in prison or something, and all he said was, "Prentiss, break out six more rods." Just like it was anybody coming down that plank.

This old woman that was with them was in charge. You could tell because she had a purse. But I started to think maybe she had a couple of loose turns on her screw, too. Come time to pay, she said something to the blind guy, and he pulled a wad of bills from his pocket. He held them straight out, smiling off into space until she pulled them through his fingers. Sure, it was nice to make the old dude feel like he was helping out, but letting a blind guy guard the money? Well, maybe it made a little sense. I mean how far is the guy going to go?

So she made them all sit down, and then she went in and paid Pud the money. I laid out their rods, leaned them on the railing just like I always do, and they all sat there like dummies staring straight ahead. All except for the blind guy. He heard me putting down the rods, and he said, "You can call me the captain," and he smiled real big. He had a big wide face and a full set of teeth, as white as you ever seen.

I thought he sounded like he was probably the only smart one in the bunch. And that would figure, him being blind and all. Sometimes they make mistakes like that up at the state hospital. Like, you know, I had an old aunt once that was real religious and they kept her up there for years until she died. Wasn't nothing wrong with her that a hot night in bed wouldn't have cured.

But when I'd sat down his rod and started going back to help Huey with the bait, he said it again, just like that, in the same voice, all deep and serious: "You can call me the captain."

Huey was back there peeling the cardboard off the boxes of cigar minnows and just laughing himself silly. "You can call me the captain," he says real serious like when I come back. And then he sticks one of them frozen cigar minnows in his ear and rolls his eyes around like a goofball.

"Huey," I said. "When are you gonna grow up?"

He just looks at me with that flat cardboard face he can get sometimes and says, "You can call me the captain."

I felt like punching him in the gut. But then Pud called back and said to throw off the lines, that we were ready to go.

It seemed kind of stupid to me to go out when we only had those six plus the four others, regular tourists, who were sitting on the other side. But like I say, it's Pud's boat and if he wants to go out, then we go out. So what if the damned boat holds thirty?

We were going out so that the crazies were on the sun side, and so I went down and told them they could move to the other side 'cause there was plenty of seats. But they all just sat there. Even the old woman with the purse. She didn't say nothing, just acted like I was trying to play some joke on them.

Then the funniest thing happened, and this is what got me. That old blind guy got up, just stood up straight as a plank, and all he said was, "Let's go." And I'll be damned if all the rest of them didn't stand up like planks, too. And the old woman led them around to the other side.

I brought around their rods and set them up again. The old man's was the last, up near the bow. And I'll be damned, as soon as I set up his rod and started to walk away, he said real quiet like, "You can call me the captain."

It was kind of spooky. And I just made up my mind to stay away from the guy.

Well, about two hours out when we got to the drop-off and Pud started gunning around trying to pick up something on the fish finder, I had to go down and put the bait in their trays. Huey always makes a deal with me. He says he'll clean it all up if I dish it out. He says it makes him feel like he's in a restaurant and he's serving up all this smelly slop to people. He says he has nightmares about it.

So naturally I'm down there slapping all that squid and them cigars in the trays when I realize all of a sudden like that I'm probably gonna have to show them all how to put it on the hooks. And worst of all, I'm gonna probably have to bait up the blind guy myself.

I mean, it can give a guy the spooks. To stand up in front of a bunch of drooling fools and explain how to put a minnow that's falling to pieces onto a hook, that's the limit you know. Like I'm some kind of a professor and they're college students.

Well, anyway, I was about to bite the bullet on this one when something happened that I just couldn't believe.

This old guy stood up again, just like a plank, like always, like the boat was sitting stock still in a parking lot somewheres, and he reaches over and grabs the rod and feels down for the bait and grabs some of that, and then he's got the hook and he's sticking the bait on the hook.

Then he turns around like he's looking at all the others and he nods at them. And them, they've all been sitting there like they're hypnotized and he's got the watch in his hand and he's swinging it so their eyes are glued to it. They just stand up like planks too and grab their rods and bait them up pretty as you please.

And of course you know by now what the old guy said after that.

Well, Pud finally found a good spot and sounded the bell to let down the lines and everything went real smooth. I was having a good time because one of them tourists was a college girl with her dad and her two brothers and I could tell that she just hated to fish. When they hate to fish you know they're looking for something else.

So she starts having all kinds of trouble naturally and naturally I'm the only one who can fix it. She gets her line twisted up in her dad's and her brothers', she gets her weight caught on the bottom and can't pull it up. And god almighty, when she catches anything, I mean even a little yellowtail, she just goes crazy and has to have me over.

So I start figuring that maybe on that long ride back, me and her might go down below for a while, like maybe she might get a little seasick or something and she might need some attention. I mean, you know Janey and me ain't been getting along too well lately. And a guy's got to feel good about himself. I mean if him and a girl are going good and then she starts to put him off it can do bad things to a guy.

Well, after a while they'd been catching a lot of small stuff and everybody seemed to be having a good time, all except the dad and the brothers. They start grumbling. I can always tell when they start grumbling and I don't even have to hear it. It's like a sixth sense I have. So I have to go and tell Pud it's time to pull up and hit one of the good spots.

I figure then it's time for me to bait up a rod. With only ten of them, there ain't a hell of a lot for me to do and so I figure I might try to hang into a grouper and pick up a little something extra for the trip. And, of course, impress the girl. That always impresses them, when you ain't fished for hours and all anybody's caught is little stuff, and then you start fishing and you catch something big. And I was starting to notice how this girl had on one of them low-cut bras, and down her shirt I could see the tops of her nipples were poking out. So I thought I'd set up my rod right next to her, if you catch my drift.

Well, I was all set to go when there was this big commotion from down the other end. It seemed like the dorky kid had hung into something big and the two big black dudes were bouncing up and down on their seats like they had springs on their asses.

And that pear woman, you should have seen her. She was turned around beating her forehead on the side of the cabin while the purse lady tried to pull her off. I mean it was a mess. And the lines were all tangled and everything.

So I straightened it all out and the purse lady got them calmed down and we all started watching him bring up the fish.

I could see it down deep at first like it was some ink in the water, way down where the green starts getting blue. And old Coke bottle, he was a sight, grunting like a hog. Damned fool nearly bit his tongue off.

Well, as it come up I seen what it was, a great big amberjack, must have been fifty pounds. And I knew that none of them had ever seen it yet 'cause they was all looking over to the side of where it was, where the line went down. You know how the water makes everything look like it's somewheres else.

So I seen the girl over there looking down too, and I thought to myself, Prentiss my boy, here is a chance to look like the god that you are. You will tell them what the fish is before they have even seen a shadow of it.

So I was about to say it real official like, amberjack, about fifty pounds—you know, say it kind of short and obvious like anybody would know it—but I'll be damned if that captain, and I'll tell you he was sitting there like a board and hadn't looked over the side once, said in that big deep voice of his: "Amberjack, about sixty-five pounds."

Well, I almost fell off the side of the damned boat. That asshole.

All I could do then was be a little wimp and say, "More like fifty, probably." But I knew as soon as I said it that I should have kept my mouth shut.

Well, to make a short story short, I gaffed the amberjack and we got it up on deck OK and after a little while of looking at it everybody settled back down and went back to fishing. All except for the dork, that is. He just sat there staring at the fish, like he was trying to stare it down or something, his big Coke-bottle glasses against that big round button of an amberjack eye that was staring up into nothing. Can you believe it? Staring down a dead fish.

Well, after a while he started talking to it. Mumbling like at first, and then getting louder. He was saying something about his mother. Maybe he thought the fish was his mother, I don't know.

But me and the girl got a laugh out of it. We was whispering back and forth about it and I thought she was real cute the way her cheeks dimpled up when she would look down at him and his fish.

I was about to give her the idea that maybe we should go down below for a little rest from the sun when I heard that captain.

"Bring the scales," he said, real formal like. "We must weigh the leviathan." I wondered if he'd been talking to my aunt or something.

Well, I wasn't just about to weigh the leviathan. I knew that bastard wanted to show me up. 'Cause I seen when the fish come up that it was more than fifty pounds and I'd been wrong. All he wanted to do was try to queer it again for me with the girl. It had taken me ten minutes just to get him out of her head the first time, with her saying, "Isn't he amazing. Isn't he just amazing." Like he was some kind of a football quarterback.

But they were all looking at me, the whole row of them, like they were a jury. "We ain't got no scales," I hollered down to them all. "We don't keep no scales on board."

The way they looked then you'd of thought I'd murdered somebody.

Then that swine Huey comes out of the cabin with the scales

and don't say a word. He just walks past and smiles real big at the girl and tosses the scales in my lap.

I didn't have no choice. I put the hook on the bottom of the scales through the fish's mouth and hauled the bastard up. It was hard as hell holding it still and I was keeping my fingers crossed the whole time. But I'll be damned if that bastard didn't stop quivering right smack dab on sixty-five.

Julie, that little college girl, jumped right up in the air. "Sixty-five pounds," she said. "Why, that's exactly what the captain said. Isn't he amazing?"

My last hope had been that they'd none of them heard what he'd said, or that they'd forgotten it.

"That's right, Prentiss, my man, sixty-five," said Huey. He was leaning in the cabin door and sucking a beer. That smug bastard.

I knew I should have drug that fish off to the ice chest as soon as Coke bottle caught it. But I was just too lazy. I figure it's their business to haul it back there, not mine. But I wasn't making the same mistake twice, so I drug it on back and tossed it in. It lay there looking up at me from the bottom of the box like it was all happy there, all satisfied. Fucked by a fish, I thought, that's what happened to me. Fucked by a fish.

When I came back my heart went sick.

That little bitch was up there by the captain and Coke bottle, right between them I mean. She had moved her rod and everything.

I remember later that night I was sitting on the dock and watching the lights over across the harbor at the liquor store flickering on and off. Huey and I had cleaned up, and he and Pud had gone on home. And I tell you what, I just couldn't go home.

I mean Janey was expecting me to be there at eight 'cause she was going to come over to my trailer and watch the Friday-night movie with me. And then I guess I could have tried again to get her warmed up. But I just couldn't. It wasn't no use.

It was like that old woman with the purse said to me when she came off the boat. I'd been getting up the nuts to ask her all afternoon, I mean to ask her about that captain character. I figured she was the only one who'd give me a straight answer.

Well, that college girl had given me a little smile when she came off and so I decided it all hadn't been that bad, but then the looneys came off and I had to ask the old woman. So when they were on the dock I grabbed her off to the side for a second.

"Say, ma'am," I said real polite like. "Tell me about that captain. I mean, is he really a captain?"

She laughed a little laugh way deep down in her throat, like it was from some kind of trouble down inside her that she'd gotten used to so she could laugh about it. "He got to you, didn't he?" she said.

"What?" I said. "Naw, I mean I just want to know. Curious, you know."

She had these little eyes that were like stones, with the lids all bumpy over them and around them. "He got to you. He gets to everybody."

"I mean was he a captain?" I said. I could see him then out of the corner of my eye. He was standing under the light at the corner of the pier with the others. They were all looking down in the water where the light shines into it and you can see the baitfish swarming. Only he was staring off above their bent shoulders, across the harbor and into the marshes where all the critters were starting up their night noises.

"Captain, hell," was what she said. And she said it real bitter. "He's never set foot on a boat in his life, at least not as far as I know."

"I mean what about the hat, and all that 'call me the captain' stuff."

"Listen, young man," she said. "You forget about him. He's straight from the devil. Anytime he goes anywhere he's something. When we go to the hospital, he's a doctor. When we go to the zoo, he's a big game hunter. You name it."

"But the fish, he knew about the fish."

"He knows about everything," she said. "You just forget about him." She didn't say another word and walked back over to where they were, and the whole bunch of them left. He passed right by me, and I was expecting him to say it again but he didn't.

He just walked up the steps to the parking lot real stiff, like a board, and his hand was on the tall kid's shoulder.

You'd think maybe that would be the end of it. But while I was standing there watching them drive off, Huey comes up behind me and slaps me on the back. When I turn around, he's grinning like a fool, that curly blond hair of his sticking out above that round face like he's some kind of a clown. "Got a little present for Prentiss," he says.

He pointed back down to the boat, and I thought he meant scrubbing the deck. With the dock lights on, the boat looked real peaceful, rocking up against the dock. The water lapped up against it, and the lights reflected off the paint in little yellow streaks. Sometimes late at night I like to come down to the water and just watch it like that.

Huey grabbed my arm and led me down the plank. "Let go of me, you idiot," I said.

He didn't say a thing. He still had that silly grin. He'd been drinking beer the whole trip back. You could smell it. When we got on board he started to whisper.

"We got to be quiet," he said. "We got to sneak up on him."

He took me through the cabin and back to the stern where there were some canvas deck chairs. I could see somebody slumped down in one of them. He was wearing a tan cap, the kind with a long bill to cut down the glare when you're fishing. I had one like it, and when we came closer I saw my name on the back where I'd printed it in blue ink. That idiot Huey had put my cap on the fish, which was propped on its tail in the chair. He had stuck a sign in front of it that read: "Call me the Captain."

Huey was doubled over laughing. "It's all yours, Prentiss," he said. He tried to catch his breath and put his arm around my shoulder. "They said they wanted you to have it." He was howling.

I wanted to strangle him, but I had to admit, it looked kind of funny, sitting there in my hat like it owned the place. The one eye of the fish I could see was still clear, and in the lights from the dock it seemed alert, maybe even a little friendly.

Creeping Things

She is lying on her back in the crawl space under the house on the cool red earth, staring at the bottom of the floor, at the nails poking through the wood, which is split around them. The cobwebs are so old and abandoned, she thinks. Only her breath moves them now. A woman in her thirties, she has taken off her clothes, removed them while her eyes were still unused to the darkness, before the damp smell of the earth became her own. She rolled and bent to pull off her slacks, the grainy dirt sticking to her back.

She wonders how long it's been since the dirt was in the sun and there was grass growing here. When she first took off her clothes she felt embarrassed. Forbidden. She crouched in the dark until her eyes became used to it. She held her clothes in front of her. Then, braver, she let them down. She crawled to the grating and looked into the neighborhood. Peaceful lawns, children playing, the old man down the street in his blue golf cap, watering his faded grass. The cool air surrounding her rushed around her face and out the vent.

This is her son's fault. It's silly to say that she's under the house because her son is carried away with insects, but she knows the truth is often ridiculous. Edgar is inseparable from the net he uses to capture them. Even on trips to the grocery store with her, he insists on carrying it, bounding across the parking lot while she is inside doing her shopping.

"They're attracted to the colors of the cars," he tells her, praising the butterflies he captures and anesthetizes right there in the front seat. When she returns with the groceries and gets into the driver's side, the odor of alcohol makes her giddy.

The cool darkness of the crawl space of the house enters her. She thinks, if I don't understand him, then I don't understand myself. I have a past here. I have a place.

"What will the police think if they pull us over?" she said to him in the car. "They'll smell the alcohol and throw us in jail as drunks."

"They won't throw *me* in jail," he said. He showed her the Styrofoam board to which he'd pinned his latest victims, a big yellow one and a tiny blue that seemed to her like a faded violet pinned to girl's white collar. "See," he said, "my butterflies are proof."

Always a slight child, now at the age of eleven he is growing even faster than the kudzu climbing the red clay bluff behind their house. Running with the long-handled net, he is too thin, too fragile to move so fast over the ground. He's a set of Pickup Sticks flying through the air, about to crash into a topsy-turvy jumble that she'll never be able to sort out.

One day in a moment of panic, she called Spencer at work. They might be divorced, but he was still the boy's father, and fathers were supposed to know about such things.

"I'm worried about Edgar," she said. "He doesn't think of anything but insects."

Spencer's voice over the phone was a piece of black velvet strewn with diamonds. "Maybe we're overreacting here," he said. "To humor youth is the grace of the gods."

"Spence," she said, "knock off the palaver. I need some help."

"What is a child but a pasture mown by the dew?" He cleared his throat. "If it bothers you, Penny, then I'm sorry," he added. "What else I can tell you?"

She could imagine Spencer's pinched face squeezing its self-concern into the mouthpiece of the phone.

"He's almost a teenager, Spencer. He's obsessed with insects. He sneaks out after midnight on weekends, racing up and down the street with his net."

"Maybe you should go back to the church," he said. "Prayer can work wonders."

"What's gotten into you?"

He was both gentle and immovable. She was Edgar's mother, he told her, a bright woman, and should know what to do better than he did.

But she didn't know. She had never known, ever since that morning in the hospital when she floated up from under the anesthetic and the nurse brought Edgar in, swaddled in a blue blanket. All through her pregnancy she'd tried to get used to the idea of the child inside her. The nurse, with an almost malicious grin, thrust the bundle toward her. Penny drew back, horrified by the baby's red wrinkled face. "There's some mistake," she said, still groggy, her stomach turning like a wobbly waterwheel.

Spencer and the nurse laughed. "There, there," the nurse said, a kindly voice erupting from the grin. "You're just a little off-kilter right now."

Penny took the baby and accepted everything they told her about it, the weight, the length, the name that she and Spencer had apparently agreed on earlier. She'd been off-kilter ever since.

If Spencer had treated her on the phone like a child, her neighbor Claudine was even less help.

"It's Edgar and those bugs," Penny said to her one day when they were both in the backyard watering their gardens. Penny was growing tomatoes, and Claudine was growing squash and beans. They would swap when the crops came in.

"Send him over here," Claudine said, her wide flat face beaming. "Something's into my squash." She paused. "It's just a phase, Penny. Remember when he was drilling holes in the backyard with the water hose?" Claudine's cheeks and forehead were red from the heat. She had thick ears that stuck out like handles. They were even redder than her face. Penny cringed to see her like that, but Claudine's skin never tanned, never grew wrinkled and old. It was a miracle, Penny decided, a miracle brought on by ignorance.

"It may be a phase," she said, "but it scares me. He's bringing in wasps and all sorts of things. Yesterday, he brought in a big black centipede that must have been four inches long." Claudine, weeding a hill of squash, hardly appeared to be listening. "He said he got it at your house," Penny added quickly, unable to resist the lie.

Claudine froze. "My house?" she said. "Where at my house?"

"Under the house."

"He's been crawling under my house!" She dropped the weeding tool. Penny hoped Claudine was having visions of Edgar under the floorboards of her house while she was . . . doing what? Talking to herself on the toilet, making love with her husband, George. Penny relished the thought of Claudine's life exposed. That would teach her not to take Edgar's strange behavior so lightly.

The centipede itself wasn't a lie, but she didn't know where he'd gotten it. He'd come in so many times with dirt all over his clothes and a wild look in his eyes as he hurried to his room with a jar in his hands.

That afternoon after talking with Claudine, she was in the kitchen having some iced tea when he rushed in, his white T-shirt streaked with dirt and a clumpy strand of cobweb stuck to his hair. She asked him where he'd been.

"Under the Williamses' house," he said. "They've got the most beetles in the neighborhood." He held up the jar and the bottom was a tumble of bugs, their hard carapaces black and brown and iridescent green. The biggest, with horns like a dinosaur, was unlike any of the others. Its huge shell was shiny gray with black spots. It climbed across the tumult of the others as if they were so many grains of sand.

"I don't want you under any more houses," she said. "You could be hurt and no one would find you."

"I'll be OK," he answered. Then he said proudly, "I know my way under every house in the neighborhood."

"Why are you so obsessed with bugs, anyway?" she asked.

He looked puzzled. "I'm not 'sessed," he said, "whatever that is." He looked down at the floor. "I love them," he said.

"But you kill them." Penny was trying to be patient.

"I don't kill them. I don't."

Penny didn't know what to think. She was more confused than ever. She packed him off to the shower and sat down at the kitchen counter, staring at the pile of his dirty clothes next to the laundry-room door. For the first time in years, she remembered that day when she was eight, playing in her yard, and some neighbor boys had called to her.

Now, twenty-seven years later, she lies under the house where the silence lets her hear, as if for the first time, the clear voices of the neighborhood, the lawn sprinkler swishing around, the dog barking, pulling on its chain, and the child's bike with cards pinned to the frame so the spokes slap them faster and faster into a high-pitched buzz.

"Hey, Penny," they say, the boys, twenty-seven years back.

"Come here." There's more than one of them calling, but she can't see them. "Psst," a voice says from Billy Henderson's house. Peering from behind a metalwork grate in the base of the house are white faces.

"Who's that?" she says.

"It's me . . . Billy," one of the faces says. "Come on over. We're starting a club."

She leaves her doll on top of the fire engine it has been riding to rescue a family, and walks over to the grating. She makes out Billy's face and Pete Donalson's and Rex Williams's. "What kind of a club is it?" she says.

"A real neat club," Rex Williams says.

She doesn't like his voice. He's always whiny. He's only five and, as far as Penny's concerned, too young to play with. But Pete Donalson she likes a lot. He's real cute, with short blond hair in a crew cut. He always wears a black T-shirt that makes his blue eyes stand out like stars.

Naked now, and alone under the house, Penny feels so large, thinking of herself as a grown woman so far from what she was. She's Gulliver in the land of the Lilliputians, thinking about those boys, so small and their voices buzzing.

"Around back," they say. "The door's under the porch."

She crawls through the opening under the back porch and closes the low wooden door. In the almost total darkness, her eyes adjust. The air smells dry and earthy, reminding her of her grandfather's hay barn in Kentucky, where she plays with kittens in the summer. In the light from the gratings, the motes of dust hover like tiny creatures in a cave beneath the sea.

Farther under the house, the boys are sitting in a shallow depression scooped from the dirt. They've taken off their shirts, which lie in a heap in the center like a cloth campfire. Penny likes

Pete's shoulders, wide and rounded over the arms. As she crawls in beside the boys, he says, "It's a secret club and I'm the president."

Penny imagines herself as the secretary, taking down the important things that Pete says. The Gulliver Penny, looking from years later, thinks of how she never really changed. Her time in college, her marriage, she was always taking down the important things someone else was saying. Now there's no one to listen to but herself, under the house in the dark cool air, her breath calm and her heart beating slowly.

"First of all," Pete says, "you have to swear that anything you see in the club is a dead dark secret." His face is hard and serious, his lips pressing tight like a pink rubber band.

Noticing how cute Pete looks when he's serious, Penny says, "Are there any other rules?"

The Gulliver Penny says the same thing, too, out loud, and wonders what someone would think if they heard her. She imagines Claudine's husband George, all 250 cake-eating pounds of him, lumbering to the grate and peering in to see her naked, the giant Penny, for the first time larger than anyone, stretched on the cool earth. Her nakedness has possessed the neighborhood, spread into the dark, hidden places, sought out the crevices, and spun its web between rafters. Then she remembers the night of her honeymoon. She was a virgin, and Spencer's body had made her seem so small.

"It's a nudiss club," blurts out Rex Williams.

The other boys give him menacing looks. They tell her what they all must do, and then they sit there, looking doubtful. But Penny surprises them. "OK," she says. She tugs off her socks and unbuttons her shirt. The boys look at one another, as if not sure what her actions mean, and then they slowly remove their pants. After removing her shirt, Penny stops and watches them.

All the boys are naked, around her in the pit. "Come on," Billy says to her. "You're not nekkid yet."

Maybe all men are crazy, thinks the Gulliver Penny. Maybe it's something in their genes that makes them get into things that shouldn't be gotten into. That day, she grabbed her things in a flash and was out of the pit, crawling fast for the door. She heard the boys scrambling behind her but she didn't dare look back. She threw open the door and fell into the sunlight.

Later, she wondered if what she'd done was a sin. The priest at their church was Father Nolan, white-haired, senile. She couldn't see him through the veil of the confessional, but she knew him from his voice, which wheezed and rustled like an accordion made of paper sacks.

"Did you enjoy it?" he said.

Did he mean had she enjoyed seeing them naked? Well, yes. It was the funniest thing that had ever happened. She'd loved that look on fat Billy Henderson's face as he cowered in back of the doorway, poking his fist into the sunlight and threatening her.

"Yes, Father," she said.

"Then it's a sin," he said. "A sin of the flesh."

"What's that?" she said.

"What?" he said. "Oh, yes. The flesh is nothing but dust and worms." Father Nolan lapsed off into the mumbling prayers that Penny knew were those of absolution. She said her act of contrition and got up to leave.

"One thing more," the Father said. "Pray for those boys who sinned with you."

Penny tried to pray for them, but all she could see was how silly they'd looked. Rex Williams's gleaming face at the grating of the house saying "a real neat club" would fade into the darkness where it would become Father Nolan's face saying "the flesh."

Older, she decided the flesh wasn't what she looked at in the mirror, or what she ran the washcloth over in the bathtub. Nor was it the body she tried to strengthen by running track and swimming in the afternoons in high school. It was a wild impatience overtaking her while she was sitting behind the steering wheel in the automatic carwash, or while she was lifting a can of peas from the grocery shelf. She thought marriage would stop it. For a while, she believed it had. Then Edgar was born. The desire she'd thought was the flesh left her. But the impatience was still there, vague and yet impenetrable. Spencer had not been able to satisfy it. Nothing could satisfy it.

Her marriage was as cold as the underside of the house is now against her body. But it was less comforting. This coldness is hers alone. She realizes the flesh is the small hard knot of self-possession that has been left to her. Here it can grow, reach into the past where it's the little boys getting her to take off her clothes without even knowing why, and it's her waiting for them to take off theirs so she can run away and make fun of them. Down here with all the creeping things under the house, the flesh can remember sitting in a barn alone with kittens at her grandfather's house. It's listening to them purr, wishing the time would never end. It's the flesh that made her want her parents and grandfather and everyone in the world to disappear and leave her alone forever.

Above her in the house, the world is going on. The washer changes into its spin cycle and startles Penny out of her reverie. Edgar comes in the back door and yells to ask when lunch is. Penny listens to the silence that her son hears as he expects her voice. His feet move across the kitchen floor, right above her face. She wonders if he is afraid, if coming home and finding that she's not where she's supposed to be has left him thinking of her in some new way, the way she saw her own parents when she first realized that one day they would die.

Edgar scrapes his feet on the floor and then runs the faucet. A glass clinks down on the counter. He yells for her again and says he's going up the block to check on some wildflowers by the highway. Then, he's out the door.

What if she never came up from under the house? The previous month in the paper there was a story about a boy Edgar's age whose mother had died in her bed and the boy kept going to school, telling no one. He'd taken all the money from her purse and bought frozen pizzas. When that ran out, he'd begged for money after school. The Gulliver Penny wonders what it would be like if the flesh weren't just dust and worms, but were immortal. She would never return from under the house. Edgar would grow old and move away. A new family would move in. On and on, until finally the house would collapse around her. The boards would rot, the grass would grow, and there she would be, once more in the sunlight.

She wishes she could go back twenty-seven years and ask those boys what it was they wanted from her. Did they think that because she was different from them, seeing her would answer something? Seeing them had only troubled her. Maybe that's all love would ever be, confusion. Her skin itches and tingles. She's a grown woman, naked underneath her own house, and it's time for her to put on her clothes and crawl out. She gathers the clothes and puts them on. A few pebbles stick to her back and she has to reach awkwardly under her shirt and scrape them off. When she has tied her shoes, she crawls to the back of the house and crawls into the sunlight. She goes in the kitchen door and climbs the stairs to the bedrooms. The door to Edgar's room has "DO NOT ENTER ON PAIN OF DEATH" signs taped all over it. He made them with a computer program his father gave him, and each has a dot-matrix picture of a skull and crossbones.

It's strange that the red, wrinkled little thing born to her, which Spencer and the nurse thrust upon her, is now this child with a personality and a life of its own.

She's not seen his collection, but she knows he keeps it in his closet in a steamer trunk. She opens the door and sees the trunk is unlocked. She has a pang of guilt and then throws open the lid.

Underneath are the glass-covered wooden trays he made with his father on weekends. The insects are carefully mounted above navy blue velvet on long, thin pins. Under each bug are pinned two pieces of paper, carefully spaced like the floors of a house, with the name of the bug, and the time and place of its capture. Penny had no idea her son was so methodical. All she has seen is the wild running, the dirty clothes, the flushed face racing through the downstairs as Edgar carries his jars of fluttering, crawling treasure. The top tray contains wasps, dozens of them laid in vertical rows, and then a big concentration of them at the lower part. She holds the tray out from her, realizing the wasps have been laid out to form a large hand. She sets that one down and lifts the next. Beetles, those she saw in the jar. The big spotted gray and black one is on the left side, with two iridescent ones flanking it.

A circle of smaller ones parade around them to make the figure of a head, a cat's head. The tail on the other end of its body is a string of black beetles. She takes out case after case, seeing a dog, a horse. At the bottom are three cases of butterflies, all formed into human heads. She knows right away who they are. Herself, dark and somber, and Spencer, a strange mixture of brightness, and Edgar, the smallest, full of the littlest of butterflies, white, and purple, and blue. Penny's deepest fear rushes into her. She has never known her son. How can she love him?

The crude portraits he has made with butterflies are hardly faces at all, and yet she recognizes them, his and Spencer's and hers. She picks up the one of herself. How had he known her so well? All the dark varieties of her thoughts, the large and the small, the delicate and the hard. Penny closes the empty trunk. The cases are all around her on the floor. They are like a circus, small and still and stopped, as if they are waiting for her to wave her hand, and like magic they will come to life.

The door to the room opens and there is Edgar, with his net at his side, and with horror rising in his face.

"Mom," he says. He is pleading for something he already knows is lost.

"Edgar," she says. "I'm sorry. I know you were keeping these secret."

He tosses down the net and pushes past her, throwing up the lid of the trunk and hurriedly putting the trays back in. "You might as well just take all the doors off my room," he says. "How would you like it if I looked in all your drawers?"

"But they're beautiful," she says. "Your insects. They're amazing. The things you've made with them."

"They're mine and not anybody else's. If I wanted you to see them I would have shown them to you." He takes the last tray, the one of her, from her hands where she sits on the floor. He stops and looks at it. Somewhere between anger and sadness, his face settles. "Did you like it?" he says. "It's you."

She is under the house, naked, on her knees kneeling in front of the vent grating and looking into the bright neighborhood. Forgive me. Forgive me for being alone.

"I do like it," she says. "It broke my heart." She reaches up to his arm and touches it. He is shaking. She helps him put the tray back in the trunk and they close the lid. Penny feels as if she has awakened, in a dark place where no one can see her. They are all around her, the host of insects, each in its quietness, listening, and her son with his net, running, scooping them from the air.

Sirens

Washburn can see them down there, their black-and-white-striped bodies turning in the current around the concrete pillars of the bridge. They're just at the edge of the flats, where the bottom begins to slope into the ship channel. They're big, the biggest he's seen in the five years since he moved to Florida. Bottom fish, some people would call them trash fish, complaining of bones. Washburn knows you can't just come out to the water and expect it to dazzle you. You have to pay attention. The tide runs across the patches of sea grass, sweeping them like hair. He can't decide which he likes more—the fishing, or the things he sees while fishing—the shadows of the clouds, the way they break the glaze of the surface, the bottom looming clear, the wandering black spike changed suddenly to a sand shark that glides between the grasses.

Unlike the crowd at the low end of the bridge who use dead shrimp and catch nothing but small worthless catfish, Washburn has come to where the bridge is near its peak, about sixty feet over the water, and he uses live shrimp. That's the real trick, the live shrimp he carries in a bucket with a battery-powered aerator. Down in the five-gallon plastic bucket, they stand on their spindly little legs and crawl around, a sort of strutting, floating motion that reminds him of astronauts in space. The black beads that are their eyes poke out from their almost transparent heads. Shrimp, he thinks, what a life.

Back in Philadelphia, the year before his wife died, one day when she'd been so sick she couldn't even get out of bed, he looked out her bedroom window and watched the yardmen working in his neighbor's garden. They were bees in a kept hive, and he was no different. The next morning, he gave up eating honey on his toast. Then he realized he was being silly. Why let all his sadness fill him with thoughts that led nowhere? You couldn't change your course for such things, not even for death. The next day the yardmen were back. They might live like bees, he thought, but they were perfectly happy, snipping back the azalea bushes, working mulch in the beds.

His wife's slow death, her breath slipping deeper into her chest until finally it couldn't reach the surface, taught him that life is more precious when things are slipping away. Still, it's a lesson he hates. He feels tied to it and fights it, although he knows it's all that keeps him going.

Washburn reaches into the shrimp bucket and scoops one up in the dip net. He runs the hook through its back. Then he swings his pole over the side of the bridge and lets the line loose, watching the weight and the shrimp glide to the bottom. Almost immediately one of the fish noses the bait. Washburn waits until it turns on its side, its tall body too high to get down to the shrimp otherwise, then he jerks the rod and sets the hook. The fish is a good one and it thrums the line, pulsing the rod up and down as it tries to get away.

The young woman appears from nowhere.

"Hi," she says. Her voice is tiny and high-pitched. He doesn't hear it so much as he feels it against the side of his neck.

Washburn is too intent on battling the fish to be startled by her. It takes a moment for the voice to register. By then she is leaning over the railing beside him, staring down at the fish, whose black-and-white stripes make it look like a dancing puffed-up clown as it struggles. She is short and has short blond hair. She's in a red bikini and has a soft, rounded figure, not fat by any means, but not thin either. She looks up at his face and he sees out of the corner of his eye that her cheeks are freckled, her eyes a washed-out blue.

"Hi," he says. He does not want to get involved in a conversation, but he doesn't want to be rude either. He adjusts the drag of his reel so the fish can take out line more easily. He wants to make sure it's plenty tired and can't struggle at all before he tries to pull it up to the bridge.

"I've been watching you," she says. "And I think you're wonderful." The words come in a breath of excitement. She holds out the binoculars hanging from a strap around her neck. "I saw you from down in the park." She points across the ship channel to the other shore where there's a small roadside park near the highway with a few picnic tables and charcoal grills.

Washburn can't help himself. He glances up from the fish. "What?" he says.

"I think you're wonderful." She smiles at him.

Before he realizes what he's done, the rod has dipped in his hands and the line has gone slack. He yanks the rod up quickly.

Nothing, the fish has gotten off.

"I've got to go now," she says. "But I'll be back." She passes behind him, stepping over the barrier between the walkway and the road, then back onto the walkway and down to where the others are fishing on the low part of the bridge. He watches her hips swinging, quick and soft, and the white bottoms of her bare feet as she moves away.

"What the hell?" He reels up the line and stares into the water, watching the striped bodies of the fish turn and dart around the pilings.

Some people think that all bottom fish are the same, and that any jerk can stand with a pole in his hand and wait for them, the stupidest and slowest of fish. Like the guy he is always running into in the condos where he lives, Crandall, that's his name, Art Crandall, who's always talking about going out on the boat.

"Let's go out on the boat this weekend and I'll show you some real fishing," Crandall will say. Crandall's a little younger, about fifty-five, with a full head of silver hair and a deep tan. He always walks around as if he's trying to push his chest up into his chin. "Last week we got into a school of amberjack," Crandall will say. "We gave'm hell."

Crandall's always getting into a school of something. And he's always saying let's go out on the boat this weekend. He stops on the bridge when Washburn is fishing. Washburn will hear a car slowing down behind him and then Crandall's buzz-saw voice. "Hey Wash, catching bait for the weekend?"

He'll turn, and there will be Crandall smiling at him, that big square tanned face.

But all bottom fishing is not the same. Some of it takes skill, a lot of skill, more skill than gunning a big boat across the ocean while you sit like Art Crandall in a chair and wait for something to hook itself.

He gazes into the bucket of shrimp and counts them. Five left. He'll have to be more careful and not let himself be distracted. He looks down the bridge to where the girl has gone and sees her talking to an old black man who's with his family.

"I've been watching you," Washburn says. "I think you're wonderful." He takes the dip net and captures another shrimp. "What the hell?" he says, shaking his head and looking again at the girl. Thinking of the white soles of her feet as she walked away, he remembers that moment when he first saw his wife Louise begin to curl in on herself. In the end she was almost perfect, a shell washed up on the beach, the white whorl of its body hard and self-sufficient.

"I think you're wonderful," he says again and rubs his hand across the top of his head, back onto his neck. Feeling how leathery the sun has made his skin, he stares into the water.

There is one big one that stays close to the pilings. You have to be careful. If you let your line down too close, the current will sweep it around and you'll get snagged. He's already broken off his line six times.

He lets loose the bail on his reel and the shrimp spins down to the water, dropping not more than two feet from the piling. Just right. Just where the big fish will see it.

The big fish . . . God, he thinks, that was what his brother was always saying, his brother who was always trying to get him to move to what he called the real Florida, Naples. You can forget anything in Naples, his brother says. But Washburn has been to Naples. He drove away from the beach until he came to the far edge of town where a few black people lived in shacks, as if they'd sunk there through some sedimentation process. Across town, floating on the white beaches by the water, where the wind blew softly through the palms, were his brother and all his brother's rich friends.

"The big fish," his brother said that afternoon, scooping peanuts from the crystal bowl on his glass coffee table, "goes to the one with the big boat."

Washburn has never understood the logic of this. On the other hand he's never been able to figure out why it's not logical. All arguments with his brother come down to that. Like Art Crandall, his brother doesn't make sense, but he can't prove him wrong.

He has finally decided it's a world of Art Crandalls. That's all he knows and all he needs to know.

A big sailboat is coming down the channel, blowing its horn like a sub on a crash dive. A couple of kids sitting on the deck near the bow, their legs dangling off, wave at the bridge. Washburn can't see well enough to tell if they're waving at him but he waves anyway. As the boat comes under the bridge he sees them more clearly and realizes they're older than he thought and they're giving him the finger. In the back cockpit is a crowd of people, all of them in fraternity T-shirts. Like the children I never had, he thinks. He has the urge to rush to the other side of the bridge and douse them with his bucket full of shrimp water.

But the fish has struck. It's the big one, turning on its side and fighting to twist free of the line. Four times it darts for the pilings but he manages to pull it back just before it reaches the concrete. By the time the fish is fought out, lying passively on its side on the surface like a painted urn, Washburn is out of breath himself. He leans on the railing.

"Is that a striped marlin?" the girl says. She's right beside him. He smells the rich, sweet, coconut tanning lotion on her glistening skin.

He laughs. He doesn't care now if the fish gets away. He has fought it to a standstill. "No," he says. "It's better than that."

"Can I take your picture with it?"

"My picture?"

"I told you I thought you were wonderful." She doesn't seem to be joking. And even though she looks young, twenty at most, the kind of perky young blond he's used to seeing around the condo pool, she doesn't act that way at all. She's calm and certain. She frightens him.

"I'm an old man," he says. He gives the rod a couple of tugs, but the fish doesn't move.

"My camera is in the car," she says. "I'll go get it."

He wants to tell her no, but instead he watches her walk toward the roadside park. He takes in his fishing rod and grabs the line at the end, pulling it hand over hand, watching the fish as it comes up. If it begins to struggle he will have to let the line go and hope for the best. In moments like these, it's better to think of something else. He pictures lying in his room on the bed and looking through the sliding glass door at the ocean. He has never understood the ocean and in fact has never wanted to understand it. He lies for hours watching the blue as it changes to green and back while the sun moves across the sky and the clouds drift over. The window of his room blocks the sound, so he imagines it as it suits him. Sometimes, on days when the surface is almost still, topped with little points of dancing light, he imagines the surf roaring. Finding that something so vast as the ocean can bend to his will pleases him. He sits on the beach and listens to the smallest sounds so he can store them up and remember them, giving them back to the ocean as he sees fit from the comfort of his bed.

By the time he's hauled the fish up onto the walkway, she's back with the camera. Her face is bright and friendly and close. She puts the camera to her eye and the lens stares at him.

"Hold it up," she says. "And smile."

He feels silly and a little weak holding the fish in front of his chest, but he smiles and she takes the picture.

"Why do you want a picture of an old man and a fish?" he says as she puts the camera back in its leather case.

"I told you. I think you're wonderful." She says it calmly, as if it's a fact anyone would be aware of.

"That doesn't make any sense. People don't go around saying that kind of thing to strangers," he says. Something in her voice makes him angry. She's not acting like a flirt, not playing a game. She has no right to sound so sure. No right to come up to him at all.

She strings the camera strap over her shoulder and looks up at him, the pupils of her washed-out blue eyes like pinpoints in the bright sun. Her body is so round and soft to him, soft earth that would give way under him like quicksand, but her eyes are different. They're hard as rocks.

"Why does it bother you?" she says. "Doesn't it make you happy?"

"Happy?"

"Don't you want me to love you?"

His mind goes blank. Then he half realizes he's still holding the fish to his chest. His thoughts are floating outside his body, he's unable to control his muscles. The fish stays there, up at his chest like a big medal, and his arms are pale ribbons dangling below it.

"Love me," he says. It's a statement, a question, a wish, and none of those.

She's walking away then, down the bridge toward her car, the camera swinging at her side under her right arm. She's small walking away, going down the slope of the bridge and seeming smaller and smaller until by the time she's reached her car, he can't focus on her anymore.

He thinks of running after her. Then he thinks of how she might return another day when he's on the bridge fishing. She'll come and tell him the story of her life. It will be sad and he'll be able to help her somehow. He'll be wise and stoic. He's a king, as she, and only she, has recognized. But no, he's not a king and she is never coming back. She has no right, he thinks, to say that kind of thing and then walk away.

Just then a young boy of about seven or eight comes up from

the other end of the bridge where the crowd has been catching catfish. He has a wide freckled face, sunburned across the nose, and wears a baseball cap with a picture of a bass boat across the front. "Hey, mister," he says, "you see that lady down there?" He points to the roadside park where the girl has just gotten into her car and is driving off.

"Yes," Washburn says.

"You better watch out for her," the boy says authoritatively.

"Why's that?"

"'Cause she's drunk!" This last word spurts out of the boy's mouth in a spasm of astonishment and wonder.

Before Washburn can say anything in response, the boy has wheeled around and is loping back to the low end of the bridge, holding on to his hat with one hand and whipping himself like a jockey with the other.

Washburn knows the girl was not drunk, but why did the boy appear before him to say so? He looks at the crowd below. They don't seem to be watching him for a response. They're back to their fishing, lined at the rail as they have been all morning. Still, someone must have told the boy the girl was drunk, and someone must have suggested that others needed to be warned.

Looking down into his bucket, the water bubbling around the air hose and the shrimp strutting along the bottom in their strange promenade, Washburn wonders what she said to them. Did she tell them that she thought they were wonderful, that she loved them?

A Spell

"to sit in darkness here
Hatching vain Empires"

The gloomy morning clouds hovered over Audubon Park like the underside of an old mattress. Shelley sat on the high, four-poster bed by the window and looked from their second-floor room at the live oak whose limbs drooped toward the balcony. You and I are two of a kind, she said to herself, the two of us always reaching. The water that ran down the limbs of the big oak and dripped to the ground was like the energy she'd felt draining out of her since she'd arrived in New Orleans the day before.

Her husband, Brent, gone for almost an hour, was making calls down at the pay phone in the dining room. The bedrooms of the Victorian guest house had no phones, and that was the first thing he'd complained about. She tried not to think about his complaining and thought instead of how she'd enjoyed breakfast in the large dining room with a fourteen-foot ceiling and a tile floor checkered white and black. It was the perfect place to have beignets and coffee, or ice cream on a hot day in the summer when the tall windows reaching to the floor would be open and you could walk to where the breeze was blowing the curtains and step right into the rose garden beyond.

It had taken her years to realize that Brent had no imagination. For a long time she'd thought he was just afraid to let it out, afraid like so many men to dream of anything beyond a career and a wife who'd love him and give him children. Finally she'd given up on trying to bring him out of his shell. He was his shell, and to think of bringing him out of it was like reaching into a mirror to get the other you.

She shuddered to think of his tall, stooped frame the evening before when they'd arrived. He walked into the wonderful room of antiques and ornate moldings and cast his scornful look upon the two beds. They were high, four-posters, that made Shelley instantly glad she'd called ahead to rent the room.

"I'll never fit on these," he said. "They're too short and they've got footboards so I can't hang my feet off. We'll have to be in separate beds so I can sleep angled across." He flung the top of his suitcase open and stomped over to his bed. He lay down and turned away from her, sulking.

"How do you think this makes me feel?" she said. "Every time I try to plan something nice, you make me suffer."

"Yeah, right!" he said. He curled up and moved closer to the window beside his bed. He probably wanted her to think he had his eyes closed, trying to get rid of her, but she knew he was most likely looking out the window at St. Charles Street. After nine years of marriage, she knew him well enough to suspect that he was already thinking about something else, probably some stock market deal for a client. Shelley opened her suitcase and unfolded her best nightgown. It was the only one she'd brought, the one she wore when she was feeling romantic. Now, it would be a cruel joke she'd played on herself.

A few minutes later in the bathroom, brushing her teeth, she could have sworn she heard Brent humming a tune, but when she emerged he was snoring lightly. He still had on his clothes. She watched him, fighting the motherly impulse to go over and take off his shoes and help him under the covers.

In the morning, before the rain arrived and settled in with its heavy gray clouds, the early sun was miraculous. It streamed in through the window and made the dark wood of the bedposts shine. Shelley watched herself in the mirror of the dresser as she lay on her side and basked in the sun spilling across the white bedspread. The room had an odd, old smell that reminded her of a down comforter her grandmother kept in the closet and brought out especially for Shelley when she came as a child to visit. Across from the foot of her bed, next to where Brent was still curled asleep, was a fireplace with a marble mantel held by two carved oak columns. Above stood a mirror which, perhaps because it was discolored and cracked across one corner, added a sense of nostalgia and romance.

She got up and walked downstairs to the dining room and had some breakfast. She was the only one eating, and the room was empty except for a fat man who drank coffee in long noisy sips while reading the newspaper. After each page, he snapped the paper from top to bottom and then folded the crease carefully on the table. By the time she finished her eggs and coffee, the man had gotten on Shelley's nerves so intensely that she had to forgo the airy warmth of the dining room and escape upstairs. In their room, Brent was already dressed and had his briefcase open on the bed.

"I have to go make some calls," he said. No good morning, no telling her how nice she looked. He picked up a manila file folder and walked to the door. "Be back in a flash," he said. He gave her his best boyish smile. She scowled at him, but he didn't seem to notice.

After an hour of waiting for him to return, she gave up and went into the bathroom, running water into the tub and pouring in the bath lotion she'd brought. It was scented with lilac. She sank into the bubbles, thinking of Brent, how the warmth of the water was like his body. She decided she would forgive him when she'd finished her bath.

As she toweled off, she heard a loud thump from beyond the door and the sound of Brent scuffling around. The bedsprings squeaked a few times. She wrapped a small towel around her wet hair and put on her bathrobe. When she emerged into the bedroom, he was sitting up on the bed and pointing at the floor.

"Look!" he said. At the base of the fireplace was a big book, opened in the middle. "It jumped off the shelf," he said. "I was lying here thinking about you in the bathtub and it just jumped off."

"So?" Shelley said.

"Well, look at it. Look at the passage that's marked in orange."

Shelley leaned over and saw that the book was a mildewed anthology of literature and that it had opened to Milton's *Paradise Lost*. She'd read Milton in college, not one of her happier times. Some earlier owner had marked a passage with what appeared to be an orange crayon. The oil had seeped into the page, making a big greasy spot. The words were from Satan's speech: "Better to reign in hell than serve in Heav'n."

"Sounds like the story of your life, Brent," she said, suddenly in no mood to forgive him anymore.

"Don't you see?" he said. "It jumped off the mantel and fell open there."

She picked it up and closed it and put it on the mantel. "So?" she said. "Now it's back where it belongs."

She thought that was the last of it, but in the early afternoon she returned from a walk in the park and found Brent in the room with two of the maids, showing them the book. He was describing how it leaped from the shelf and fell open to the exact place of Satan's words. The maids were astonished. The young one, who was over-weight and had a flat baby face, stepped back from the spot on the rug where Brent said the book had landed. The other leaned cautiously to read the words in the book, which Brent was holding in his hands. When she finished, she said, "Sho nuff is," and told Brent she was going to call an aunt of hers right away to come over and see if there was any spell on. The aunt was a teacher, she said, and might want her students to see it, too. Just then, the manager bristled into the room. He was a plump red-haired man with an of-ficious manner. While Shelley was taking breakfast in the dining room earlier, she had heard him on the phone speaking in a thin gossipy voice about someone named Di. Intrigued that he might be on to the latest about the royals, she had immediately tried to listen in, but she was disappointed. Di was only the name of some cat that had been wreaking havoc on the manager's settee.

When he saw the two maids standing around, the manager crackled at them. "Girls, now girls," he said, "we can't be acting like this is a tea party, can we?"

"Look heah," the older one said. She pointed to the book. "Tell Mr. Higgis what happened," she said to Brent.

Brent told again what happened and Higgis's eyes opened like two pale blue flowers. "My stars," he said. "We might have a real thing here. We might have a haunting."

Shelley couldn't believe her ears. The four of them launched into a frenzy of speculation. Their voices rattled and chirped like the wheels of rusty tricycles racing down a hill. The older maid, whose name was Charmante, dashed from the room to call her aunt. The manager took the book from Brent and held it with what could have only been called reverence, as he turned it carefully in the light to examine its faded spine.

By late that afternoon, the room was a circus sideshow. Every fifteen minutes or so, another knock at the door, and one of the maids or Higgis would bring in an admiring enthusiast of the occult to hear Brent's growing rendition of the miraculous event. The story came to include a strange choking sensation that Brent felt, just before the fireplace gave forth a low eerie groan and the book sprang from the mantel. The book did not fall open to the page, so much as the pages blew there by the force of some unfelt wind. By later in the afternoon, Brent had recalled how just at that moment, a beam of sunlight broke through the window to illuminate the page. Oddly, though, the light had not come from the eastern window, as one would have suspected in the morning, but from the west, which was otherwise full of dark menacing clouds.

Shelley could not contain herself. If it hadn't been for the downpour, which had begun again and which had not let up though the afternoon, she would have escaped. Higgis had a lot of nerve, she thought, using Brent's silly story to try to drum up interest in his guest house. The stream of locals and other guests intruding into the room was bad enough, but it was Brent who infuriated her. He would not refuse to let them in. Even more than the book itself, he had become the object of their admiration. For the women especially. Shelley watched from her bed while an unbelievable group of rain-soaked women, who were in a reading club Higgis belonged to, raised their glowing faces to Brent's and heard the ridiculous tale. After he added the part about nearly choking, they even began to want to touch him, their dripping hands reaching furtively out and the fingers sliding across the tops of his.

"Why don't you go down to the lobby and watch TV if it bothers you," he said when she told him for the fifth time how upset she was.

"What!" she said. "And leave you with all these ghoul groupies?"

He laughed. Sitting on the bed beside her and putting his arm around her waist, he pulled her to him and kissed her on the temple and on the cheek. "Aren't you always telling me I'm a stick-in-the-mud?" he said. "I'd think you would be happy to see me like this. It's great. I haven't had so much fun in years."

"It's crazy," she said. "You're making a fool of yourself."

"I'm just telling what I saw."

"The next thing you'll be telling them is that Satan appeared in the fireplace."

"Well, now that I remember, there WAS a kind of a glow there." He grinned at her. "Don't worry," he said. "Let's just have fun. After all, this is a vacation."

"Some vacation. We sit in a room and watch the rain dripping from tree limbs while one kook after another parades through the door."

"OK," he said. "We'll go out. We'll get the umbrella and catch the trolley."

As they left, Brent insisted on darting into the manager's office to tell him they were going out for a while. They were on a first-name basis, Brent and Doug, which irritated Shelley even more. From the hallway, Shelley watched the street through the elegant beveled glass of the door and felt her enthusiasm for going out die as she listened to the hushed excitement of their voices. When Brent returned, he was bubbling.

"You'll never guess who's coming tonight. It's Madame Touselline. She's a voodoo queen. She's Charmante's aunt."

"Oh hell," Shelley said, and she jerked the door open, rattling the glass. As they walked onto the porch she caught a glimpse of Higgis sticking his putty face nervously into the hallway. For years she had dreamed of getting Brent to a romantic place like this, and now look what had happened. Brent had changed all right, he'd become like Higgis, a sick mushroom who thrived on dampness and oddity.

They had a long wait for the trolley that ran down St. Charles, but the big umbrella they had borrowed kept them dry and the cool fresh air made Shelley feel better. It was romantic to stand under the wide live oaks in the rain with Brent next to her, holding the umbrella over her. She hugged him close and he put his arm around her. When the trolley came, they got seats on the side away from Audubon Park and Shelley gazed in wonder at the elegant houses that they passed as they traveled toward town. Brent had learned the directions to a well-known restaurant from the manager. By the time they finished dinner she had completely forgotten about the horrors of the afternoon. Brent was in a better mood than she had seen him in a long time. As he laughed and told jokes, she realized how much his work had gotten to him the last couple of years. Although he was still young, his face had hardened. It seemed so fixed, so determined. But as they sat in the restaurant, drinking champagne and having their dessert, a flaming platter of bananas in a chocolate liqueur sauce, she felt as if they were on their first date together.

When they came out of the restaurant, the rain had stopped and the night air was washed in the faint smell of flowers. They were both giddy from the champagne, and they decided to walk back to the guest house. It was only about a mile. They could take their time and look at the Victorian houses that had impressed Shelley so much before. Back on St. Charles, they watched the trolley go by, its windows lit and its passengers lively. Most of the people had probably been drinking, and they were going up and down St. Charles to one bar after another, enjoying the Friday evening. Shelley was glad she and Brent were taking the slow way back. As she gazed through the windows into the graceful hallways and living rooms of the houses along the street, she imagined herself living at the turn of the century. That was her time, the time she had always known she was suited for, when women surrounded themselves with a tasteful elegance and men did not dare to disturb it.

When they reached the guest house, a tall, late Victorian structure of four stories with balconies and cupolas, Shelley felt she was about to step into her natural home, as if she'd been born there and was returning after a long time away. They went up the steps onto the front porch and she imagined that instantly a butler would appear to open the door for them. He would know her and would welcome her home with all the graciousness and dignity that had been long overdue to her.

Brent opened the door. There was a shout from down the hallway and a crowd of people came rushing forward from the lobby and the manager's office. Higgis maneuvered to the head of the crowd and was pressed into Brent by their forward movement.

"You're back at last," he said. His voice was filled with exasperation and delight. "I had to practically put them all in chains to keep them out of your room. Some of them are from the Society." He leaned over to Shelley and Brent, and whispered, "They investigate everything." His eyebrows rose. "Everything," he added.

A tall thin white woman dressed totally in black loomed over Higgis's head and touched Brent's hair with a frilled pouch that appeared to have been made from part of a Persian rug. "Ask him about the voices, Doug," someone said from deep in the hallway.

Higgis raised his voice. "Now everyone, there's going to be time for all your questions. Let's make way so Brent can take you to the book."

Shelley found herself abandoned at the doorway while Brent was hurried up the stairs, the crowd of people pushing after him. There must have been twenty-five of them. Shelley wondered if good old Doug had been on the phone all day calling them, or if they'd just picked up the news on some psychic airwave. Rather than follow, she went into the dining room and sat at one of the tables. The room was dark and she could see out through the floor-to-ceiling windows into Audubon Park. It was so peaceful. She wished she could take one of the four-poster beds from their room and put it under a big spreading oak tree and sleep there in the park, dreaming of the houses along St. Charles.

She waited for what seemed like an hour and then she went into the lobby. God only knows what he's telling them by now, she thought. She pictured Brent acting out the devil's appearance in the room, flames shooting from the fireplace and the book itself also on fire, although it did not burn. What had gotten into him, she wondered. Maybe there was something strange about the book, but it wasn't what they thought. It was what the book had done to Brent. As she climbed the stairs, two teenage boys came down, whispering in awed tones. They squeezed past her on the middle landing, and she caught the eyes of one of them. The boy didn't seem to see her. He was in a trance with the other one, as if they could see and hear each other but no one else.

The door to the room was open. Many of the crowd had left, but there were still about ten kneeling on the floor, surrounding Brent who was standing in front of the fireplace with the book open at his feet. They were all rocking back and forth, like mental patients, Shelley thought. They listened with rapt attention to

Brent. He was telling about his college days. It was ordinary stuff she'd heard a thousand times, but they were enthralled, as if he were telling them about a mystical experience.

"What in blue blazes is going on here?" Shelley said. Brent looked up. The rest of them didn't seem to hear her. "Hey," she said. She gave Higgis a nudge in the rear with the toe of her shoe. He shook his head and then slowly turned to gaze up at her. "Enough is enough," she said. "Get out of here, all of you." Brent leaned over and tapped the people closest to him. In a couple of minutes they were all standing, moving dreamily toward the door. The manager was apologetic. "The room's free," he said. "For as long as you want to stay." His little blue eyes penetrated her like ice picks.

Shelley slammed the door behind them. "Brent, you're an idiot," she said. She flopped onto her bed and closed her eyes. The springs of the other bed squeaked as Brent sat down. For an instant she thought she never wanted to see him again. He could take his little sideshow, his little newfound life, and could go to hell with it.

"I'm sorry, Shell," he said. His voice was tired and distant. "I guess I got carried away. Can you forgive me?"

She didn't open her eyes. It was better in the darkness, with her head pressed down into the thick feather pillow. He didn't say anything else, and in a while she fell asleep.

The knock at the door was like the sound of a bucket bobbing in the water against the sides of a deep well. She was a little girl and had been sent there by her grandmother to draw up some water. But instead of turning the crank of the well, she was opening the door. The light in the hallway was bright and the two women were like black statues against it.

"This is my aunt," Charmante said.

Shelley couldn't focus. She made out Charmante's face, but the other woman, who was taller, was indistinct. She glided around Shelley and into the room, near the fireplace. Brent was sound asleep. The glow from the streetlamps came in through the window and cast him in a pale light that flowed and darkened from the rain running down the glass.

"I am Madame Touselline," the woman said. Shelley could see her more clearly. She was younger than Charmante. Her hair was full and vibrant. She had on a long cape, and as she drew it back Shelley thought of a warrior, tall and powerful and sexual.

"It's late," Shelley stammered. "I was asleep."

"I know," Madame Touselline said. "I came to stop all this nonsense." She looked down at Brent's curled figure on the bed. "Men are swine," she said. She walked to the mantel and pulled down the book. She held it in front of her for a moment as if she were meditating on it. Then she held it over Brent. Shelley thought she was about to drop it on him, but Madame Touselline swung the book like a divining rod toward Shelley. She walked closer. The cape dropped from her shoulders and her lithe body swept behind Shelley, who felt paralyzed. The woman was a good six inches taller than she was, and her long arms encircled Shelley, holding the book in front of her. She felt Madame Touselline's large warm breasts pressing against her as she moved up and down slowly. Shelley's heart was exploding.

"The power is yours," Madame Touselline said. Her voice rumbled, like the engine of a freight train on a steep grade. "The power is yours," she repeated. She raised the book over Shelley's head, then stepped away from her. Shelley's legs went soft, and Charmante grabbed her and set her on the bed.

"What was that all about?" Shelley said, coming to her senses.

Madame Touselline swept up her cape from the floor and

marched to the mantel, tossing the book on it. "You been lettin' this man jerk you around, sister. And that's just all there is to it," she said. With that she strode to the door and was gone before Shelley could collect her thoughts. Charmante sheepishly followed and closed the door behind them softly.

Shelley lay back on her pillow. She felt as if Madame Touselline had reached down through her mouth and pulled out her insides. New Orleans was gone, all the spreading trees, the park, the trolley, the houses with their beveled glass windows and doors. Where had she and Brent lived all these years? She couldn't remember. Was it in a house? Or had they just hovered in the air, like two spirits, confused by each other and yet drawn together by some force they couldn't see? Madame Touselline's performance had shaken the room, rattled the beds and the windows, made the floor roll like the ocean, and yet Brent had not awakened. He lay sleeping, still curled on his side, snoring peacefully. Was he innocent? Was she, Shelley, the one who had always made things difficult by her selfishness, by her insatiable desire to live another way? Or was Madame Touselline right?

She closed her eyes. His snoring was a luffed sail in a thin breeze. Still hearing his breath, she sensed that he had gotten up. He walked across the room and stood over her. His knees pressed down the bed at her side. She opened her eyes and he was over her, his bare chest swelling and the muscles of his arms thick and tense. "Brent," she said. There was nothing boyish about his face anymore. She grabbed his arms and threw him over. Rolling on top of him, she put her hands around his neck. It was hot, like fire, and she felt the blood under the skin, fast, the pulse of a rabbit.

The Robber

"Have you been waiting long?"

On peaceful days I look down from the third-floor bedroom onto the low marshy ground and the saw grass, and beyond into the shallow flats of the bay where a stingray glides, a brown shadow, the wings of its body hardly moving, a slow undulation of the water. The mullet are different. In schools of twenty or thirty, they swim quickly, as if they're going somewhere, although after a while they return, the same school, the two big ones in the middle, shifting in and out, two so large they look like parents of the rest.

I'm here to learn patience. Although you might say I am here to die. I don't know what I will die of, the doctors don't know, at least they can't tell me. Maybe I'm not dying. No one has said I am, but I can feel it. Nothing definite, nothing that catches up with me suddenly, just a slow emptiness that moves in and out like the tide.

The man who sold me the unit, who said it was a good investment, drove a dark blue BMW and had little patience. He had come to north Florida, he said, from Sarasota because everything was going to hell in Sarasota. Although he was ten years younger than me his skin was like leather, like a wet brown shoe left out in the sun, my wife would have said. He poked his tanned arm and said, "A month down here and you'll be like me. Fighting the widows off with a stick."

I told him I'd have to think about the apartment.

"Take your time. But remember," he said, "the world is full of thinkers."

My wife, whose name was Christine and who died three years ago, would have had something to say to put him straight. She was always better than I was at that kind of thing. She would have spotted him even sooner than I did for one of those people who would rather not know what they are selling you.

Two little girls, down on the pier now, lie on their stomachs and look into the shallow water. I watch them in the afternoon. They come home from school, seven years old and nine, getting off the yellow bus that comes ten miles down the coast road, and running, two sisters who have lived in the apartments as long as they can remember. The oldest, the one with light brown hair that is straight and long, likes to say she remembers when they lived on an island where there were hula girls. Maybe it's true. The other denies it, the serious one who reminds me of Christine. Her hair is short and curly, but that is not what reminds me, it is her cheekbones, high and red under her large blue eyes when she says, "Adelaida is lying, Mr. Paulka, we never lived anywhere like that."

Adelaida goes on, like the salesman who has no patience with the truth, "And there were men who played little guitars and put strings of flowers around our necks."

Suppose it's true. Imagine the dreams you have of your past are true. The girls' parents are in the service and work at the air force base. They could have lived in Hawaii, too long ago for the little one to remember.

"It's not a lie," says Adelaida.

At first, the saw grass and the marsh. Then beyond that a margin of sand, a long fat snake of sand separating the marsh from the clear waters of the bay. Where the girls are looking into the water, it's no more than a foot deep, the bottom sandy, the little holes of burrowing animals like tiny volcanoes in flat desert. Farther out, large spots of sea grass, ten, twenty feet across, and then the water deepens and the solid beds of grass begin.

Christine said, "You struggle all your life, Al, and where does it get you?" She was at the breakfast table in the kitchen the day before she died. She had on the pink bathrobe with the white trim, the one I didn't like too much. But it was the warmest one she had, and the day was cold.

"I don't know," I said.

"Patience," she said. "That's all there is."

It's funny I even remember it, that whole conversation at the breakfast table. It's not like it was the last thing she said. She wasn't even sick. The next day she went to the hairdresser, came home, fixed dinner. Then after dinner there was some heartburn. In the middle of the night she woke up, and we knew it had been an attack.

There was time to say a lot of things, about worrying, about taking care of myself. She did it all. But I don't remember much of that.

I see that the little girls have a stick. They are chasing a crab, trying to move it into the shallower water, up close to the beach so they can catch it in their bucket.

The frost on the window. In the kitchen it was like a tiger stretched out on a bed of rocks. "Patience?" I said.

She was stirring her coffee with the little spoon she always used, the silver one that was barely long enough to reach the bottom of the cup. Her thumb and forefinger, holding the spoon, formed a small, almost perfect triangle. "Think how long it took us to get here," she said. "All the billions of years the earth was forming."

"What's gotten into you?" I said.

"I've been thinking," she said. "You know how I get sometimes."

I knew she was beautiful. I knew I loved her most when I saw her lost in thought, sometimes in the strangest places, like in the grocery store one time. She was in front of the frozen foods, and I came up beside her because I saw that she had stopped. What is it, I asked. And she told me she had felt something she couldn't describe, something beautiful. She didn't need to describe it, I could see it in her face.

In the kitchen she stirred her coffee, on and on, as if she would not stop.

"All those years," she said. "How much did it hurt us to wait to be born?"

"None, I guess. We were dead."

"That," she said, "or maybe it was patience. Maybe we knew all about patience then and now we've forgotten."

"That's horrible," I said. "Like we were alive and couldn't do anything but wait. How can you think about a thing like that?"

She didn't say a thing and kept on stirring her coffee.

It made me mad as hell when the priest gave his sermon. He said we all had to think, we had to realize how death could take us at any time. He told them all how she had been to the hairdresser and had come home happy and fixed dinner. He had no right. He used what I had told him, had told him crying in the hospital.

When I went to the bank to take out my money, I told the woman I was going to Florida. She was a plump young woman with her hair bleached and long paste-on fingernails, orange nails that matched the lipstick she was wearing. "Do you want a check?" she said.

"I'll take the cash," I said.

"I'll have to tell the manager," she said. "Anything over ten thousand dollars and I have to tell the manager."

"So tell the manager."

She snatched up the papers in her long fingernails and swung her hips as she walked into the manager's office. I waited while he signed the papers. I could tell he was flirting with her. They were laughing.

"Sorry to keep you waiting," she said when she came back. She counted out the cash, and I gave her a brown paper bag to put it in.

"Just like a bank robber," I said.

She laughed, but she didn't think it was funny.

When she handed me the bag I looked her straight in the eye.

"We've all forgotten how long it took us to get here," I said.

She smiled at me, and her fat cheeks spread out like two little pink hams. She said, "Have a nice trip."

I went straight from the bank and cleaned out my house. I threw it all away, the furniture, the things my wife had worn. A neighbor boy helped me drag it all out to the street, everything except a steamer trunk and two suitcases of my own things. The boy, who was only sixteen but had a big strong back and on his forearm a tattoo of a snake holding roses in its mouth, kept calling me a wild man. "Hey wild man," he'd say, "what about this?" Then he'd point to something else in the room. A month earlier he would have made me mad as hell calling me that.

We got to the hall closet last. He was worn out, lying on his back at the end of the hall, and I was in a rage, dragging out the steamer trunk, cutting grooves down the floor. He whistled and said, "Hey wild man, what's your rush?"

His red hair fanned around his face like a stripped cedar wreath. He was staring at the ceiling, not even looking at me, as if he were talking to the air.

"Nothing," I said. "No rush."

"Then what's your hurry? Slow down." He raised his head and looked at me. His eyes were little green beads, cheap jewelry. "What's in the trunk?" he said. I didn't know. We opened it. My wife had packed it, years and years of mementos.

I wanted to stop at the first layer, but the boy kept pulling things out. At the bottom was the gun. My old service automatic. I hadn't touched it since I came back from Italy. Along the side, just above the trigger, was a big rusty thumbprint. I held the gun in my hand and put my thumb right over the print.

The gun changes things. No one sees it. No one ever knows it's there. That's not the point. The gun is all about patience. It stays under my jacket. For all I know, it will stay there forever.

Are you in line with me, are you waiting? There are forms to fill out, there's a ticket to buy. Then another line.

The gun changes that. There are no more lines, there's only patience. You're standing with all the others but you feel it in your pocket and then you're looking out on the bay, watching the fish glide through the water.

The girls have managed to get the crab up onto the beach and they have a milk carton to capture it in. A quick swoop of the stick and they have it. Adelaida holds the carton in her upstretched arm like a torch of triumph and they run down the beach, to the clump of gnarled, windblown trees that they've made their hideout. Inside is an old hammock, a couple of lawn chairs with half the webbing gone. They raid the Dumpster whenever anyone moves out. Treasure. An old toaster, a clock, a rug with a picture of a stag, all sandy, worn down by the weather, hidden. Except that everyone knows about it, anyone who walks down the beach can look into the clump of trees and see what they have put there.

In the same way, Christine is hidden from me. The gun can't change that, the gun is only about patience, about controlling the end of things. I have countless victims. The roads are littered with them, the banks, the grocery stores, the hospitals.

"Didn't take you long to make up your mind," the real estate man said when I went into his office later in the afternoon.

I smiled at him and put my hand over the gun. "It's a steal," I said. "I'm stealing from you."

He laughed. "You're gonna love it," he said. "The water right there outside your door. You like to fish, don't you?"

"I'll learn," I said.

"You'll have all the time in the world," he said.

Flying St. Croix

Down the road from the airport was the horse-racing track, its wooden fence gone gray and the grass beneath the stands growing up through the bleachers, as if the structure were sinking and the island's soft green were slowly absorbing it. Ray and Shaunelle strolled through the high grass along the fence to peer into the overgrown track, and then they settled down near the road, where a peeling sign marked the entrance. From his nylon traveling bag, Ray pulled out the bottle of local rum he'd bought in the airport with his last two dollars and opened it. He poured some into their soft drinks.

"Shaunelle, my love," he said, "let you and I partake of the nectar of the gods."

Shaunelle, for her part, was sick of hearing him talk like that. After only an hour, she was sick of being on the island. She was sick of hearing the refined and musical accents of the native islanders. She was sick of the beautiful weather and the land that was so green and rich it made her feel as if she'd just eaten two pounds of pecan divinity.

Most of all, she was sick of Ray. He'd done nothing but praise everything since they'd arrived. Even at the airport in Puerto Rico, when they'd left the big jet they'd taken from Philadelphia and transferred to the small prop plane that would take them to St. Croix, his enthusiasm was percolating.

"What an adventure!" he said, strapping himself into the hard plastic, bucket seat beside her. There was a short row of seats on each side of the narrow aisle that led to the pilot's cabin, a cubbyhole of blue lights and switches. The red plastic curtain that separated the cubbyhole from the passengers was ripped at the top and it hung like the cape of an ill-fated toreador. She and Ray were seated by the wings, which seemed to her like twigs held together by the metal beam that ran across the cabin floor at their feet. The captain, a round dark Puerto Rican with a huge smile, came on board and addressed the passengers in Spanish.

"*Gracias al Gordo,*" he said, making the sign of the cross, *"nos vamos en seguida."* With that, he made a hedgehog-like shuffle into the cabin and jerked at the torn curtain, pulling it momentarily over the hole and then letting it fall to the side where it had been.

Moments later, the engines cranked up, spitting blue smoke. As they revved faster, the engines and their short blades seemed ineffectual, like four angry wasps held by pins.

Ray's eyes were polished black buttons. He thrust out both thumbs and jerked them up and down like the man on the ground crew beyond the window. The plane bobbled forward. Then it was gliding and the motors grew even louder. The wasps turned to hornets. Still pinned, they were dragging the cardboard plane across the ground. Shaunelle tried to swallow her stomach back to where it was supposed to be.

The plane shot onto the runway behind a huge DC-10 which was lumbering toward the terminal. Then, they swung hard to the right and almost instantly the plane gunned forward, the little wisps of its blades screaming and the wings bucking. They lifted from ground uncertainly and then banked up and to the right. Hanging sideways over the window, Shaunelle saw the long strip of hotels along the beach coming toward them. The engines strained and the hotels dropped away. The plane leveled and the coastline came straight. Off to the west, old San Juan and the *castillo* sat like a cluster of child's blocks strewn at the edge of the sea.

"You are now leaving the land of Roberto Clemente," Ray said in a jubilant voice. In the fifty minutes that they'd actually been on Puerto Rican soil, waiting for their connecting flight, Ray had become obsessed with baseball, rattling off to Shaunelle the names of all the famous players who'd come from the island. His hero was Clemente, who he said died in a plane crash while on a rescue mission carrying food and clothes to starving children. "I think it was somewhere here off the north coast of the island that he crashed," Ray told her excitedly. "Just think of it." There were many times when she couldn't understand Ray. He was always getting excited over the oddest things. Whether it was a baseball player's tragic end, or a large butterfly caught in the windshield wiper of his car, she'd learned the things that set him off usually had some combination of grandeur and death, which to him was enthralling and to her, merely dismal.

He was riveted to the window, watching the clear waters beneath them, as if he might actually see Clemente's plane. Maybe even Clemente's body, Shaunelle thought, a baseball bat still in his hand. She pictured Ray asking the hedgehog pilot to circle so he could leap from the plane into the water, his long dark legs scissoring him down to the wreckage, and then his triumphant arm, breaking the surface, the bat clutched in his dripping fingers.

To her horror, when they reached the island of St. Croix, there was just such a wreck, not in the water but beside the airport in the underbrush. As they made their approach she saw it, laid out like a blackened cross. "Ray," she said, "look at that wreck." She pointed down, but he couldn't see it from his side.

"What?" he said. "You mean the airport?"

"No, the plane, a wrecked plane just like ours."

Airports were always surrounded with old planes like that, he told her, adding confidently that it wasn't a wreck but was only being stripped for parts. Descending, their plane swayed back and forth like a sheet of paper settling to the ground. The wheels chirped hard as they hit, and the whole plane bucked. Then they were down and speeding along the runway. Shaunelle released her grip on the seat. Ray had already taken off his safety belt.

"We're here!" he said. "The land of milk and honey!"

"If it was the land of milk and honey, then why was your great-great-grandaddy so all-fired hot to get out of here?" Shaunelle said.

"I told you about that. After the old plantation system broke down, there weren't any jobs. That was before tourists."

It never failed to amaze Shaunelle how Ray could twist history like a candy cane, a perfect red and white goody, hanging in its place in a stocking over the fireplace at Christmas. For all he knew, his ancestor had been a rapist and a murderer. No, she thought, that couldn't have been it. She looked at Ray's hopelessly optimistic face. His ancestor had probably been run off the island for an excess of unjustified happiness. She imagined a group of sour, unemployed sugar workers in the dead of night, hoisting the old loon in a net into the hold of a steamer, watching as the smiling face disappeared from view. The whistling and laughter echoed up from the deep chambers of the ship.

What was worse, Shaunelle was fighting the suspicion that the real reason for the trip was not, as Ray had told her, to find where he had come from. She prayed he wasn't going to try again to romance her into having a baby. He'd promised her not to mention it anymore until she was ready. He knew that after helping raise all her younger brothers and sisters, she was desperate to be free of that, at least for a while. I'll be too old to play with my child, he'd say. Sometimes Shaunelle had the sickening feeling that maybe she was avoiding a child just so she could see the sadness on Ray's face, like a secret part of him that only she could bring to life. Or maybe, even more frightening, she was avoiding a baby because she didn't love Ray enough. They'd only been married four years. Was it over already? No, she kept telling herself, her doubts weren't because of him. Was it wrong to have a life to herself, just for a little while?

Once they'd landed and gone into the terminal, even Ray had to dampen his enthusiasm. Their bags did not come off the plane. The attendant, a wiry old man with a limp and a stutter, whose white eyebrows rose ominously whenever he tried to say the word baggage, said their things would be on the next plane.

"When's that?" Shaunelle asked.

"Now, princess," Ray said, "no need to be getting upset."

She hated the way he flared his nostrils when he was being condescending to her. She wished she could shave off that little elf attendant's white eyebrows and stuff them up Ray's nose.

The old man pulled a bent and greasy schedule out of his pants pocket and handed it to her. "You may have that," he said. He smiled at her and stood there, like he was expecting her to invite him to dinner, she thought.

Ray snatched the schedule from her hands. "It'll be here at six," he said.

"OK," she said, "we'll go into town and get a room."

Ray looked down at the floor. "Uh, sweetness," he said, "don't be getting mad now, but I think maybe we should stay here."

"Why's that?" She didn't like the sugar look that was coming over his face. It was his "I'm going to sweet talk my way though this" look.

He squirmed and weaseled for a minute, and then she got it out of him that he'd put all their traveler's checks in his suitcase. Together, all they had were a few dollars.

"You butthead!" she shouted. There was a burst of wings flapping, and everyone looked up to see several startled birds whirling frantically back and forth under the ceiling of the terminal. Two of them ran into each other and fell stunned to the floor near Ray and Shaunelle. They were small green birds, and they flopped on the tiles as a crowd gathered around them.

"Stand apart," a voice said. It was the old man. He made his way to the birds, leaning over and sliding them with a whisk broom onto a piece of cardboard. As he walked away, the crowd was transfixed. Shaunelle thought he was taking them to the door to release them outside, but when he came near the door he veered to a trash barrel and threw them in it. Several women in the crowd gasped as one.

"Necks broke," he said as he walked past them. He brushed a few tiny green feathers from the cardboard, and they drifted to the floor.

The crowd moved away slowly, silently. Shaunelle had a rush of guilt. If only she hadn't yelled.

"I need some air," she said to Ray. They walked toward the door. As they came close to the trash barrel, a boy of about fourteen with dreadlocks who'd met them at the entrance earlier trying to sell postcards, came up and looked in it. He reached down and picked up one the birds and held it in his palm close to his face. He appeared to be breathing on it lightly or murmuring something to it. He wore a bright blue-and-red-flowered scarf wrapped around his head and another just like it around his upper right arm. He was like a young pirate with a baby parrot in his hand.

Shaunelle slowed as they passed him and wanted to stop, but Ray took her hand and pulled her through the door.

"You don't want to look at it," he said. Once, she'd cried all day when he ran over a field mouse in the car.

Outside the terminal, the air was balmy. The breeze lifted her spirits. Far in the east, some thunderheads had puffed themselves into the high blue sky. Ray ran back inside and bought soft drinks and rum. Then the two of them walked away from the airport. That was when they found the old racetrack.

It was an hour later, and they'd finished most of the rum when they saw someone coming down the road toward them from the airport. The bright scarf around the head and the arm. It was the boy who'd picked up the bird. His dark ebony skin was shining in the afternoon light.

He turned from the highway and came down the sand and shell road to where they were sitting. Under the arm with the scarf, he carried a cardboard box. On it was written in elaborate calligraphy: *Justin McDowell: Paradise Postcards*. The letters had the appearance of a gray silvery powder, as if woven from strands of Spanish moss. He was whistling as he approached them, not a tune that Shaunelle recognized, more of a random series of notes full of an exuberance that filled her with dread. Another one, she thought, another loon like the one they'd lowered into the dark hold of the freighter. The islands were full of them.

"Welcome, welcome," he said as he reached them. "I, Justin McDowell, am at your service." Taking the box from under his arm and holding it before him, he bowed.

"We don't have any money," Shaunelle said. "That's why we're sitting out here. So beat it." Hearing the boy's elegant, artificial voice, she felt malice rush from her like the flashing beam of a spotlight, radiating over him, shriveling him in its brilliant circle of scorn.

He seemed unconcerned. The fierce light of his teeth and eyes only shone brighter, with more happiness. "Ah, then," he said, "you are here to stay."

"We left our money in our suitcase, and it didn't come in on the plane," Ray said. "The money should be on the next flight. We're staying a week."

"Supe-e-errbb," Justin said, drawing out the word into a dreamy song. He set the box down at his feet. "Welcome to my home," he said and spread his arms wide.

"Do you live in town?" Ray said.

"No, no. I live here. Here!" He stretched his arms again, taking in the racetrack.

"You live here at this abandoned track?" said Shaunelle.

Justin did a little dance and whistled a few notes. "Here, and here I stay," he said. "Me, and the mother, and the sisters, all three." He bowed, smiled at Shaunelle, and winked at her. "Come along," he said. "You'll meet my mother." He reached for their hands to help them up. Ray took the offered hand, but Shaunelle crossed her arms and remained sitting. A happy pirate, that's what the boy was. He would have them walking the plank in an instant if there was a place to do it. He'd nudge them with the saber and smile the whole time.

"Ray," she said, "let's just wait for the plane, OK?"

Ray came around behind her and grabbed her under the arms, picking her up. She had her legs crossed like an Indian and she didn't uncross them, so that he was left holding her in the air.

"Put me down," she said, "before you get a hernia."

Justin laughed. "The lady's in a sitting mood," he said. "Never

"Nothing to worry yourself about," Justin said to his mother.
was picking with his fork at the spine of the fish he'd been
ing. Shaunelle had noticed the precision with which he'd sepa-
ed the meat from the hair-thin bones. "Ray and Shaunelle are
friends, and friends understand everything. Isn't that the
h?" he said, staring straight into Shaunelle's eyes. His pupils
huge and dark, like holes she could fall into, except that
were two of them, so as she started to tumble into one, the
pulled her away.

f course friends try to understand each other, Shaunelle
ght, but the whole thing was so ridiculous. It was the rav-
f a couple of children with overactive imaginations. And
e didn't know what was stranger, the silly ideas of the red
nd the blue one, or the serious denial of the yellow one. She
red if the last girl didn't believe it even more strongly than
ers.

u are thinking," Justin said. "But I'll tell you anyway that
er was no magician, he was a saint." Justin's face glowed
ide. "He died before the sisters were born, two years be-
y were born, but they are his. No one believed it until my
made the doctors test their blood."

elle looked to Felicia, expecting some reaction, but she
g there as calmly as if Justin had merely commented on
er.

s amazing," Ray said. "It's a miracle, then. A real live
He stared at Felicia with awe.

lle had to turn away. She might have known Ray would
ith them. He was just as crazy as they were.

low bow was looking at Ray with a fierce hatred in her
s tight. Shaunelle was suddenly relieved. The girl had

disturb a lady when she's in a sitting mood." He motioned to Ray.
"Come on," he said, "let's be getting something to wet that throat.
The lady can rest here."

She watched them walking off. Just as they crossed the track
and reached the grassy infield, she jumped up and ran after
them.

On the back side of the track were the old stables. When they
were closer, Shaunelle noticed wisps of blue smoke coming out
of a pipe extending sideways from the wall at one end. Then she
heard the singing. It was weird. The voice didn't sound human. It
made her think of a large, trapped bird.

There was no door left on the stables, but a piece of green
canvas was draped over the opening. At one end of the long hall,
where the individual stables opened out like the dark niches of
catacombs, hung another piece of canvas. The singing came from
behind that. Justin led them forward and lifted the canvas to re-
veal a neat, clean living space. The wide boards laid over the dirt
floor were damp as if they'd just been washed. Gaily colored pieces
of cloth had been nailed as bunting around the edges of the ceiling. The photos and paintings spread along the walls made the
room seem not so much like a stable claimed for a house, but more
like a family home that by some strange turn of events had had a
stable built around it. The stable had never belonged there and
was now returning to dust.

It was Justin's mother who'd been singing. She was bent over
a cast-iron stove, stoking a fire and adding some dried cane stalks
to it. She was a very thin woman with a light complexion, somewhere between brown and gray. Almost, Shaunelle realized, like
the color of the wood in the stables.

Justin spoke rapidly to her in a dialect that sounded like
English but was incomprehensible to Shaunelle. It was beautiful

and flowed from his mouth like a rapid chant. His mother smiled at him and nodded her head.

"You are invited," Justin said. And then, as if in an afterthought, he said, "to a meal you won't forget."

"No, thank you," Shaunelle said. "We need to be back at the airport." Ray's face fell, and he stepped between her and the boy.

"We'd love to stay," he said. He reached behind him and took Shaunelle's hand, pressing it in his. Staring at his back, his wide shoulders under the tan, sweat-stained shirt, she felt as if she were suddenly blocked by a mountain that had flown in her way. She wanted to jerk her hand loose and pop him a good shot across the back of the head. Just then three young girls entered the room, Justin's sisters, she supposed. All of them wore short blue dresses and white shirts. Their hair was tied behind with a ribbon, each a different color, red and blue and yellow. They were about ten years old, identical triplets, and Justin rushed over and proudly introduced them, as Jacqueline, whose ribbon was red, Françoise, blue, and Marquesa, yellow. Shaunelle wondered if Justin really knew them by their faces, or if he had to go by the ribbons, a question that was immediately answered when he looked at the ribbons and began to scold the girls.

"Playing your tricks again, I see," he said. "Now, who'll the boys be kissing if they don't know who's who?" The girls giggled and looked at one another, putting their hands over their mouths as they smirked and looked wide-eyed at Ray. Justin untied the ribbons from all three girls and switched them around. "Now there," he said, "say hello to the nice lady and gentleman who have come to visit us. They're from the United States and have come a long way to see us."

In unison, the girls said hello. Ray blew them a kiss, and they shrieked with delight and ran from the room. Shaunelle was torn

between being charmed by the beauty and cuten[e] girls and being disgusted with Ray for being so h[ ] proud of himself.

Later, sitting at the table with them and e[ ] felt guilty being so irritated with the McDow[ ] poor. They were so unlike her own family, an[d] reminded her of her own younger sisters who[ ] dinner consisted of a few small fish Justin said[ ] the morning, some mangoes, oranges, and so[ ] grown in the small garden plot beside the sta[ ] ish and praised Justin's mother, whose nam[ ] way of fixing the fish in a sauce that had a[ ] Ray insisted to Felicia more than once that[ ] the recipe, even though it was the last thin[ ] he mentioned it, Justin's mother laughed[ ] told him that the recipe was nothing.

"It's nothing but love," Justin said.[ ] winked at Shaunelle. "My mother kno[ ] went on. "She learned it from our fath[ ] who was loved by everyone."

"He could make horses fly!" shout[ ]

"He could make people come to[ ] the red bow.

The yellow bow sat silent for a [ ] Then she said with great solemnit[ ] in magic, either."

The other two scowled at her.[ ] buried him, but he didn't die," t[ ]

"Now, girls," Felicia said. "D[ ] a little frightened at what the gi[ ] that Ray and Shaunelle had he[ ]

been telling the truth about not believing. At least Shaunelle had one friend among the loons.

Ray laughed and looked at Shaunelle. "Maybe that's what it takes," he said. "Maybe after I'm dead, then we'll have a baby."

Shaunelle felt the horror rush over her. So her suspicions were right. He'd brought her on this romantic trip to the islands so she'd give in and have a baby for him. And even worse, he was sharing one of her deepest secrets with these weird strangers. She picked up the plate in front of her and slammed it down on the table, shattering it. Ray's smile was still frozen on his face. He seemed to be trying to bring it down, but the muscles were locked. She jumped up from the table, and before anyone said a word, she threw back the curtain and ran outside.

Although it was nearing seven o'clock, the sun was still fairly high, and the waves of hot air were shimmering over the corrugated tin roof of the racetrack bleachers. Shaunelle headed for the road back to the airport. She expected Ray to come out at any minute to try to calm her, but he didn't. She realized he didn't come because he knew her too well. He had tried calming her enough to know she would only get madder.

As she reached the road, a plane was taking off from the runway at the end farthest from her. It was one of the little four-engine planes like the one they'd taken from Puerto Rico. She stopped beside the road to watch it slowly climb, heading straight toward the mountain that blocked its way. She had a sudden thrill, not a fear but a strange happiness, as she thought it was going to keep going straight, right into the mountainside. But at the last minute, when it seemed that the nose of the plane must have already been touching the treetops, it pulled hard to the left and skimmed along the side of the mountain and then past it, sailing out toward the ocean.

It made her think of Ray, how he was always rushing toward things. How he rushed toward her. She couldn't help what she was, any more than the mountain could help standing in front of the runway. The comparison tickled her as she thought of Ray, kneeling naked on the bed in front of her ready to take off.

It's not my fault you built your damned runway in front of a mountain, she said, laughing to herself.

It was farther to the airport than she remembered, but as she walked, a cool afternoon breeze dried the perspiration from her face. Once, a car stopped and the man inside asked her if she wanted a ride. He was an old man in a beat-up orange Beetle and didn't seem to want anything except to be friendly and help her. When she said no, he smiled and chugged away, with blue smoke puffing from his exhaust. Shaunelle wished suddenly that she had gone with him, off into whatever life he had. Just to see what it was like to be someone else. She pictured a small shack painted blue like the smoke of the exhaust, up in the hills under the lush green trees, and a yard of rich black earth packed down hard with chickens clucking around and pecking here and there. Still, it made her sad to think she might leave Ray. She remembered breaking the McDowells' plate. How could she have done such a thing, she wondered. The McDowells were so poor and had so little. Her anger at Ray had done it. That anger had been growing in her. It was her secret baby, put there by Raymond Henry III and now feeding on her and on him, too.

By the time she reached the airport, she was more cheerful. She hadn't noticed before how clean and fragrant the island air smelled. It was like the ocean and a dozen flowers mingled together and sweeping back and forth with each new breeze. There were a few cars leaving the airport, but none coming in, and by the time she reached the terminal it was almost deserted. She looked around for the little man who had swept up the birds, but he was nowhere to be seen. She checked the desk to see if their bags had come in, but they hadn't, and then she sat down in one of the plastic chairs in a row by the front wall and wondered what she should do. The thought crossed her mind briefly that if their bags had arrived she could have gotten the traveler's checks, booked a new flight home, and been gone, leaving Ray to figure out his own way back. Maybe there would have been some poetic justice in it. The old loon, his ancestor, had been shipped off to America, and now she was returning the favor by returning his one remaining offspring, dumping him off for them to contend with. She imagined a whole tribe of rotating loons, shuffled in the darkness from country to country, their irrepressible smiles like moons rising and setting.

Instead of pleasing her, the thought saddened her. She couldn't be too hard on Ray. While she had half a dozen brothers and sisters to carry on the family, he was an only child. She'd always felt sorry for him when he wanted children. But love had to be more than feeling sorry for someone. Ray had to realize that having children meant more than just building his runway in front of a mountain and crashing into it night after night waiting for some miracle to happen. No, you won't die, you'll have a child instead. Well, it didn't work that way. The dead having children, the nerve of that Felicia McDowell, making up something like that and telling it to her children. Why didn't she tell them who the father really was and just get on with her life?

Shaunelle had had enough. She was going to get up off her rear and get back to the racetrack and tell the whole bunch of them off. And then she was going to get Ray and tell him a few things, too. She was going to tell him that she used to love him but she didn't anymore. She was going to tell him why. It was that stupid happiness of his, and it was his blindness, and it was him building his runway in front of her mountain. She wanted to love him. She ached and longed to love him. But she . . . well, that was enough. That was what she would tell him. And then she'd listen to what he had to say for himself before she said any more.

When she reached the racetrack, a few white birds were wheeling in the sky behind it, coming down into some large trees on the edge of a hill, over which the sun was setting. The face of the hill was already in the shadows, but some of the birds were up where the light could reach them, and their wings turned alternately gray and white as they rode the air down. The temperature hadn't cooled much from the sun setting, but a warm breeze had come up and was rustling the palm trees by the track entrance. She walked quickly past the stands and back to the stables where she expected to hear them all laughing and carrying on. It sickened her to think of Ray sitting around with the McDowells. It was as if he'd found a new family.

"If that's what you say you want, you can damned well have it," she said. Back when they were dating she'd always wondered if it was right to think of marrying anyone so different from herself. But whenever she saw his smiling face at her door, she couldn't help but feel uplifted. Often in the winter when she'd become depressed because of her job in the real estate office, or because of her mother being so sick and close to death for so long, she would call Ray just to hear his voice for a few minutes. Not that she especially wanted to see him, it was just that some unexplainable energy came across the phone and healed her. Being married to him was different. There was no way to get away from him. There were times when she just didn't want to be healed.

As she entered the stable where the family lived, it was quiet. She walked to the end of the row of stalls and pulled back the curtain. The dishes were still on the table, but no one was around. She went back outside and listened for their voices.

"Ray!" she shouted. "Hey, Ray, I'm back!"

She heard a thumping from the stables on the far end of the track and walked toward it. The grass was high, and she was afraid of snakes. She didn't know if the island was like Ireland where there weren't any snakes, but she didn't want to take chances. She found a place where the wooden railing around the oval track had fallen down and stepped into the raceway where the grass was thinner. At the other end she stooped under the railing and walked quickly through the high grass to the stable, whistling loudly and scuffling her feet in the hopes that maybe the snakes would hear her and get out of her way.

There wasn't much light in the stables. The damp smell of rotting wood and the sweet smell of hay rushed around her as she leaned her head in. She pulled open the creaking door to its widest and called in.

"Ray, are you back there? Justin?" The noise of heavy feet moving came from the end stall on the right. "OK, you guys," she said. "This isn't funny. You've had your little hiding game. Now come out."

The sound of a horse whinnying shocked her so much that she lost her footing and fell against the door, which swung wildly before she balanced herself.

The horse intrigued her. In spite of the dim light, she walked back to its stall. It was a beautiful roan, with big black eyes that seemed so happy to see her. It was nodding its head and reaching its mouth out across the top of the stall door as if expecting a treat.

"Aren't you lovely," Shaunelle said. She rubbed its long hard forehead and ran her hand around its ears, feeling their silky warmth. Then she noticed there was a saddle on the horse. "Oh, Ray," she said, realizing that he must have set the whole thing up as a surprise for her when she returned. He knew how much she liked horses and how she had ridden them as a child when she lived in the country. It had always bothered her that her parents had uprooted her and moved to Philadelphia. So many times she had spoken to Ray about moving out of the city. Stroking the heavy, muscled neck of the horse, she realized that one of the things she had grown to hate the most about Ray was how much he loved the city. Not that he wouldn't have loved the country just as well. To him it was all the same, and he couldn't see how for her it was different.

Now, she felt angry at him. The horse was a bribe.

"Well, old boy," she said, half to the horse and half to Ray, "this may be a bribe, but I'm going to take it anyway." She opened the stall door and reached for the reins, which were draped over the horse's neck. The big roan stomped its front hooves in anticipation. The energy flowed from it, as if the horse would burst out of the stall and over her if she didn't act quickly enough. Taking the reins, she led it from the stable and mounted into the saddle.

It amazed her how familiar the saddle felt. How long had it been since she was on a horse? Fifteen years? No, it was more like twenty. She gave the horse a nudge with the stirrups and felt its broad chest heave and shift as it bolted forward. She took it at a trot around the track once. The air was cooler now, and there was just enough light left to let her see that the birds had settled into the trees on the hill. She thought of riding out there, just leaving Ray and the McDowells and the missing luggage all in the past. The horse, as if reading her mind, rounded the turn into the straight-away and broke into a gallop heading toward the hill. Shaunelle's heart raced. As they came into the end of the straightaway, she shifted her weight for the horse to turn, but it didn't. She pulled the reins, but it kept going toward the fence. She lunged for its neck with her arms as it flew over the railing into the high grass surrounding the track.

"Damn you!" she screamed at it. The horse bucked, and she held its neck tighter, almost slipping off the saddle to the side but then getting her balance. She straightened and took the reins, holding them tightly over the neck as the horse charged past the stables into the field beyond. "All right," she yelled in its ear. "If you want to play, we'll play." She dug her heels into its flanks. It seemed to know she'd taken control and its gallop became smoother, its legs no longer as bunched, but stretching out, flying over the grass.

They were nearing the foot of the hill when she noticed a large spreading tree and beside it the remains of an old sugar mill, like the turret of a buried castle. She had seen a picture of one in the tourist brochures, but the mill was always the same one, so she'd figured they probably didn't really exist except in some park where one had been preserved. She wanted to stop and see it. It was leaning as if it had sunk into the ground and the grass was growing partway up its side. As they swept past the tree she tried to pull up the roan and turn it toward the mill, but it bolted toward the low hanging limbs of the tree.

A limb was right in her eyes, and then, nothing. In the dream, because later she realized it must have been a dream even though it seemed real, she awoke inside the turret of the sugar mill, staring up at its open top, as if she were at the bottom of a well. The grass and moss beneath her was cool and soft. Her clothes were gone and the man with her, lying naked beside her with his strong shoulder and arm beneath her head, was not Ray. The man's smell was a quaint fragrance of earth and dry flowers. She felt safe with him. He was serious, and she'd never felt so loved as when he turned and moved on top of her, taking her breasts in his hands and gliding his thumbs, which were as smooth as a baby's skin, across her nipples until they ached and rose up hard.

But when she woke in the deep grass of the field, this time really waking, it was Ray who was beside her, not naked, but beside her in exactly the same way, cradling her head on his shoulder and arm. They weren't inside the sugar mill but under the tree where she'd fallen. The roan horse was standing docilely next to them munching on the grass.

"Oh, thank God, thank God," Ray said when she opened her eyes. "Oh, my sweet, sweet Shaunelle. I thought I'd lost you." He brushed some bark from her forehead where the limb had hit. She winced from the sting as his fingers delicately cleared the embedded pieces.

"My Ray," she said, staring up at him. The moon was up behind his head, past the edge of the tree, a thin smile of a moon that was nothing like him, nothing like the Ray who was above her crying, his tears dropping onto her neck. He was different than before. She'd never believed he could hurt so deeply for her. As she kissed him, she wondered if love always needed the fear of losing someone to make it real. There had been times when she had wanted to hit him or scratch him or break something of his that he cared about, just so she could see if anything could make him see her as she really was. Pain needed company. And now, as she listened to the sobbing of his voice, it seemed that she was no longer alone.

Later, back in the McDowells' stable, putting the horse away, Justin brushed close by her, and she thought she recognized the smell of the man in her dream. Earth and dry flowers. She believed then that the man who'd made love to her was Justin's father. Not alive, but dead. The smell of the cemetery. It surprised her that this didn't trouble her. It would have earlier, when she thought Justin's mother was a fool for lying about the sisters' true father. Now, she realized that people needed their dreams. And what was wrong with that? Maybe the most love could hope for was to make a person's dream, no matter how absurd, actually happen. She and Ray rubbed the horse down. He put his hand over hers as she stroked the currycomb through its hair.

After they had tea with the McDowells and went off to the stall where Felicia McDowell and the girls had put down a blanket and sheets for them on the straw, Shaunelle took off Ray's clothes, slowly without speaking. She took off his trousers and stroked his legs and the smooth curves of the arches of his feet. She took off his shirt and felt the rise of the muscles in his chest above his ribs, and finally, taking off her own clothes while he lay still and watched her, she turned onto her back and became the mountain again. But this time it was different. He didn't crash into her or veer off into the sky. He lifted her up. They were flying, the mountain rising with him, the tiny plane, soaring over the ocean and away.

The Palm and the Cat

The day of Wiley's thirtieth birthday the hurricane came, in mid-November when he and Diane thought the season was over. When the last storms had passed, he rowed out to Post Island. The big royal palm that stood at its center was no longer there. Pulling the skiff up on the sand, he walked through the brush and saw how the wind had broken the base of the trunk, more than three feet across. The wood was crumbled like sawdust. He remembered how, when he was a kid, his cousin Mack told him the palm was at least a hundred years old. It lay down through the short pines and scrub like the long rough finger of a giant, pressed into the sand.

He'd come there to bury the cat. It was a panther, a male, and Wiley's pet, although he'd never called it anything except the cat. It had died during the hurricane, but with no sign of how it died. There were no marks on it. Its cage on the highest part of the hummock, next to the cabin, was above the curving line of weeds and limbs that marked the closest reach of the storm tide. The cat was just dead, that was all. There was no explaining it.

Sitting on the trunk of the big palm, Wiley rested from the long row to the island and looked out over Florida Bay. It was fourteen years since the night they'd found the cat.

He'd never seen a night like it, at first clear, then a storm coming quickly over Florida Bay, thunderheads pouring up heavy and dark across the evening sky. The wind blew the rain almost horizontally. He and Mack lay flat in the skiff, and the rain went right over them. The wind blew the skiff, too, sideways like a puck on ice, but it didn't even stir the water, only spit the top of it off into foam. Then the storm was over, as quickly as it had come. The dark clouds moved on to the west and left the full moon behind, just rising in the east. And something Wiley had never seen, a rainbow in the night, a white rainbow without colors.

"Look there," Mack said, pointing in the opposite direction, across the water toward the nearest island. He hadn't seen the rainbow, at least he had made no sign of it. The flat water lapped lightly against the boat, like a drifting echo of the storm.

Wiley recognized the land as Post Island, higher than the other islands, with the one big royal palm in the center. They were miles from the inlet that led to their camp in the Everglades.

"What is it?" he said.

"Can't tell. It's swimming towards us though."

Wiley could see in the moonlight the trail fanning out on the stilled water before he could make out the thing itself, a small dark head just above the water.

"Gimme the light," Mack said.

Wiley handed him the flashlight, and Mack swung the beam at the moving head. Its eyes shone back a bright gold.

"Damn," Mack said.

Wiley had been living in the camp all summer with his cousin Mack, ever since school had let out, when he'd told his father he was sick of learning and didn't want to go back in the fall. His father said nothing about school when he told him. His father was standing outside the shack, whipping some reeds to break them down for weaving. He stopped and then twisted the reeds in his hands, the big hands that had always frightened Wiley when he was small, the skin red, laced by scars. He only said, "This summer you go out and live on the island with Mack. He gon' teach you a few things." Then he went back to whipping the reeds against the post.

"Damn," Mack said again.

"What is it?"

"If it ain't a cat, I'll eat it," Mack said.

By the time they reached the cat it was nearly drowned. Mack grabbed it by the neck and hauled it in, and they saw how young it was and that it was black on its tail and along its backbone, a mass of black spots that separated and then faded lower down the panther's back, giving way to the tawny color it would be when it was grown.

"Throw it back in," Wiley said.

"What for?" Mack looked up from the cat, which lay in a wet lump on the floor of the skiff, too tired even to try to shake the water off itself. Except for its fierce eyes, it was like a muskrat with long bony legs.

"Just throw it back in."

"It's no good to kill one," Mack said. "Better luck if you don't kill it."

"I'll throw it in," Wiley said. He got up and moved toward the front of the boat.

"Throw it in, and I'll throw you in with it," Mack said. He had the oar swung back as if he meant something. Wiley sat back down.

"You wouldn't knock me in." Wiley tried to look determined. "You haven't got the nuts," he said.

"Better you than the bad luck." Mack spit into the water. He didn't act mad. He was calm. The cat was making a small noise, halfway between breathing and whimpering. Its head was down on the bottom of the boat.

"Aw hell," Wiley said, "that thing ain't going to live anyhow." He nudged its side with his toe and the cat didn't move. Its eyes were open and they looked up at him. Even though they were tired and the cat's body was limp, they still looked fierce.

But the cat didn't die, at least not for years. The cat and Wiley's father would both die in the same year, when Wiley had gotten married and given up on living alone on the isolated hummock in the shack beside the cat's pen. He knew there was some connection between that, and his father, and the death of the cat, but he didn't know what it was. On the day after the hurricane when he went to Post Island to bury the cat, he lay down on the still damp trunk of the fallen palm tree and thought how his father was in the ground, and now the cat would be in the ground. All he could see, though, was what he'd seen that morning when he looked out the window—Diane, his wife, in the yard. She shook out the wash and hung it on the line.

That night fourteen years earlier, the dim white rainbow, which had appeared where the storm had gone, had faded before Wiley remembered to point it out to Mack. Good thing, he'd thought, no telling what Mack would have wanted him to do, no telling what kind of luck would be mixed up in that.

"We got two more traps to check," Mack said. "That storm done us some good. They're right close."

"Lucky for that moon," Wiley said. It had come up high over the island, lighting the water, and he was glad to be in the boat, out on the open water with the fresh smell in the air after the storm.

Mack rowed the boat over, and Wiley snagged the white Styrofoam blocks they used to mark the crab cages, white with a blue stripe. He pulled up the rope, and at the bottom was the wire-mesh trap, almost full of crabs.

"Look at that," Mack said. "Luck's better already, and we ain't had that cat ten minutes."

"Damn, Mack," Wiley said. He looked into Mack's close-set eyes and thought of him as a possum, eyes like a possum's and too dumb to do anything but play dead. "Those crabs were in there before we ever saw that cat."

"They knew."

Wiley laughed. Then Mack laughed.

Wiley knew Mack was too serious about luck, and it made him glad to hear him laugh. Luck was something you had to laugh about. Wiley had learned that much on his own.

His father had sent him to learn from Mack, and Mack was nothing but old-fashioned and superstitious. Mack was like his father, Wiley's uncle George. Wiley remembered the afternoon after his mother died, when they'd made the long trip by skiff to Dimm's hummock, which was higher than any of the others, the one where all his family were buried. Wiley's father had wanted to take the airboats, but Uncle George, who was the oldest, had refused. It was only good if you did it the old way he had said. Wiley was ten and had only seen the graveyard once before when his grandfather died. Almost lost in the underbrush, the cement crosses were like fat tent poles holding up the brown palm leaves that had fallen over them. While the others looked for a place to bury his mother, Wiley watched a line of ants, thousands of them, carrying twigs and dead insects from the woods into their nest in the white sand at the foot of a grave. He wondered how they'd made it into the middle of the glades. Then he remembered that once, in a storm, he'd seen what looked like a whole colony of ants floating on a pile of sawdust. Nearby, his uncle was probing the sand and peat with a long metal rod, looking for the pits in the rock beneath, where the limestone marl had dissolved and left a hole deep enough to bury someone. His uncle found the place, and the others began to dig. Wiley watched them turn up the loam. They were lucky that the water had eaten the rock away. There was no way you could dig into the rock, not even with a pickax.

The cat was lying still, maybe dead, in the bottom of the boat as Mack rowed them to the last trap. When they emptied the trap they saw that the last three had given them more crabs than all the rest put together. Wiley shook out the blue crabs into the gunnysack and then baited the trap again with mullet scraps.

"Beer money," Mack said. "Good-time money."

Mack put his back into the oars, and the skiff shot across the water toward the inlet. It would take them a good thirty minutes to get back to the camp, so Wiley leaned against the bow of the boat and rested his head, looking up at the stars. Mack breathed evenly but deeply as he rowed. The oars hit the water with a smack. For a while Wiley had thought Mack was crazy for not wanting an outboard. They were so much faster, he'd argued. He remembered how Mack sat on the porch and finished his beer without saying a word. Then he tossed the can clattering off the edge of the porch and said, "It ain't the money. That ain't it. It's just that when you go fast you start thinking fast."

When Diane was young she was always thinking fast. From the day when they were kids and first started talking about getting married, she was thinking of things for him to do. She'd been born in a shack just like him, and when they were little they used to think alike. But it was her idea for them to quit high school together and go to Miami. While he spent the summer with Mack, she went to Miami and took a job in a big department store selling perfume and scarves. She wrote him every other day and put a different perfume on the letter each time. She said it was so he wouldn't forget her. After a while the perfumes smelled alike to him. None of them smelled like her. He wrote to her and told her, and she quit writing for a while. The summer was almost over. He was getting ready to come back from living in the camp with Mack, and he was supposed to go then to Miami to find a job and be with her. But she quit writing, and then he didn't know what to do. The cat was healthy by then and had put on weight so that its ribs didn't show. Its coat was sleek, and Wiley would take the cat out of its pen and sit on the ground under the big pine tree and stroke its fur. The cat's clean sharp teeth in the pink gums reminded him of Diane. He didn't know why. He'd stopped trying to think things out.

"When's Diane coming back?" Mack said. The oars didn't miss a beat. He was not out of breath, but he spoke between breaths, like "When's Diane . . . coming back?" as if the two parts of the question were two different questions.

"I don't know. I think she's mad at me for what I wrote her."

"What's that?"

"Nothing."

"Nothing?"

"Nothing I can explain."

"She'll come back," Mack said. Then a breath, a stroke of the oar. "If you want her to."

She hadn't come back, and he hadn't gone to Miami. He hadn't gone back to school either. He'd gone out to the cabin to live alone with the cat. It was September when he heard from her again. In the letter she mentioned that someone named Roy was giving her rides home from work. By Christmas she'd married Roy.

The boat was approaching the island where the camp was, and Wiley lifted his head, looking first at the cat, which lay very still beside the middle seat of the boat and then at Mack, who didn't seem to have tired at all. The boat was gliding through the water at the same even pace, the oars smacking the water, not as if moved by Mack's arms but as if they were pulled down and then pushed up by the water.

"What are you going to do with that cat?" Wiley asked.

"Not me," Mack said. "You."

"Me?"

"It's your luck. I already have my luck."

Wiley looked into Mack's possum eyes and saw nothing, no sign that Mack was joking.

"I don't want any luck from that cat."

"You don't have to want it. It's yours."

The cat would live almost fourteen years, its coat changing from spotted black and tan along the back to the sleek and tawny coat of the adult, shining in the light as if it had just been oiled. Opening the door of the big pen he'd built at the edge of the clearing for the cabin, Wiley would go in to change the water in the trough, although the cat rarely drank. And he would go in with the small animals he'd trapped for it. He liked to go in and rub the fur under its neck and along its sides and back, behind its ears, and in the depression between the heavy U-shaped bone of its lower jaw.

Luck. His father sent him to the camp for the summer to be with Mack and to learn from him, and all he'd learned was that luck was what a guy had when the traps were full of crabs and it was what he had when his girl went to Miami and stopped writing him. To Mack it was all luck. Trust it, and then you could call it good luck. Don't trust it, and then it would always be bad, even when things turned out right. Luck confused Wiley. He could look into Mack's beady eyes and see it there, luck, so simple and ignorant, like a possum playing dead.

They were almost to the pier and Wiley saw the cabin through the pines. Under the full moon the square white pine box with a slanted tin roof shone between the shadows of the trees. It looked to him as if he could walk up to it and lean down and lift off the top of the small box, letting the light into it so he could see what had been left inside.

"You can start building the pen for the cat tomorrow," Mack said.

Wiley hoped the cat wouldn't live, and he wasn't about to start working on a pen for it. It had begun to shiver, and the shivering made it look even more sickly. The bones of its shoulders poked up as if only the skin was holding them in place.

"You can build one big enough so when it grows up it can have some room."

They were at the pier and Wiley reached out to the first piling and grabbed it, pulling the skiff in and sliding it down to the second piling where he tied the bow rope, wrapped it three times and then used the knot his father had shown him. He jumped up on the pier and looked down at Mack, who had put the oars in place along the inside of the boat and was leaning over the middle seat to get the sack of crabs.

"I ain't building no pen," Wiley said.

"I'll get the crabs, you get the cat," Mack said.

"I ain't building no pen."

Mack threw the bag of crabs onto the pier. The crabs inside scuffled and clamored, their shells clacking against one another.

Then Mack was standing close in front of him, and Wiley felt a strange fear in his chest. It wasn't a fear like the one he had from the storm coming fast over the bay, it was more like the feeling when he sent his last letter to Diane, thinking about Miami, a place he'd never seen, and trying to imagine her there.

Years later, the day she returned to his father's house, he'd almost forgotten Diane. It was early in the summer before he turned thirty. His father had had the first stroke a few weeks before and the old man was in the living room, lying on his side, staring out through the screen door the way he had since they brought him back from the county hospital. Wiley and his cousin Bill had tried to get the old man into the bedroom, but he began to whimper and his right eye got wild, so they took him to the couch and he rested there easily. Day and night he lay there, slightly curled, staring out the door, even when it was so dark you couldn't see past the doorway.

"Yoo hoo," she said, Diane, stepping onto the porch, and Wiley knew it was her before he heard her voice, almost as soon as her feet touched the first of the wooden stairs leading to the porch. He thought later that maybe he had smelled her, that faint old familiar smell, because she was not wearing any of the perfumes of her letters.

He rushed out from the kitchen where he'd been washing the dishes from dinner. "Diane," he said, smiling at her as he saw her on the other side of the screen door.

He knew from her smile that everything was back to the way it had been.

"It's been a long time," he said. He unlatched the screen door and let her in. She crossed the room to where his father was on the couch, bending over him and brushing back the hair from his face.

"I heard," she said.

"It happened last month," Wiley said.

Diane stood up straight and turned from his father. She put her arms around Wiley and kissed him, running her hands behind his neck and pulling his lips tight against hers.

When she loosened her hold on him and pulled her lips away she walked quickly to the door and opened it, turning.

"I'm back now," she said. Her voice seemed harsh and out of breath, like the voice of someone standing over you after a long fight. "And I feel the same way about you I always have. I never did quit on you. I just had to slow down enough to see it." She walked across the porch and jumped over the steps onto the ground. Wiley watched her as she walked down the road and out of sight where the road turned through the pine thicket.

It was never in the daytime but only at night when Wiley heard the cat pacing. Then he would go out to the edge of the clearing beside its cage and lie on his back on the pine needles, looking up through the trees and listening. To his own breathing and the breathing of the cat as it paced the length of its cage. A patient insistence in the air. Not like the wind, coming from somewhere else, but rising from the air itself in its stillness. He would lie on his back listening and he would fall asleep, taking the sound into his dreams, which were always peaceful but left him always in the morning with the feeling, as he awoke into the light, that he was suffocating.

On the pier, Mack standing in front him, the bag of crabs rattling at his feet, Wiley was able to think of nothing but the air, the warm night air, and the decaying smell of the vegetation washed up along the shoreline. He couldn't focus on Mack's face. It was a blank space in front of him. Then he and Mack were struggling, rolling on the pier. He had no idea which one of them had started it. They'd come together at the same time without realizing what they were doing. Rolling across the pier like two men whose clothes were on fire, he and Mack both tried to get a solid hit into the other's ribs. The blows glanced off. Their hands bled from hitting the boards of the pier instead of each other.

Then they were in the water, the shallows near the shore, and the mud was all over them and they were sucking it in with their breaths and spitting it out, still locked to each other with one arm and striking wildly with the other. They realized. This was no fight. They were not fighting each other. This was crazy, nothing but blind crazy action. They were laughing. They stood up and the mud dripped off of them.

"You and your good luck," Wiley said laughing, his sides hurting, not from the blows but because he was out of breath and he couldn't stop laughing.

"You and your cat," Mack said. "Love at first sight if I ever seen it."

They climbed onto the pier and lay on their backs, catching their breaths. Swarms of mosquitoes buzzed around their heads, but the mud stopped them from biting. Wiley touched the drying mud over his face and he felt as if he'd sunk into the earth, like he was wearing it around him and nothing could touch him.

Mack laughed again. Wiley looked over and saw the figure of mud, his twin, its two eyes like the only human thing left. "We ought to get out to the highway and put up a sign," Mack said. "Swamp creatures . . . five dollars a look."

Wiley rolled his head back and gazed at the sky. The moon was above them, even a little to the west, starting to go down. There were a few clouds around it, dark ones, and it lit up their edges so he could get a sense of the tops of them, up where the light hit them straight on. He hadn't thought about the way a person could see things like that, how it looked from up where the moon was.

That afternoon years later when Diane had come in, back from Miami, he watched her walking away down the road and turned back into the room and saw his father lying on his side on the couch. He knew then that long ago he had stopped seeing his father. He saw only an old man on the couch, a carving that didn't change. Like the picture of Diane in his mind all the years since she'd left. Even before she had left. He'd never really seen her, only an image of her. He went to the couch and sat down on the floor in front of his father and ran his fingers through the old man's hair, still dark and thick, in spite of his age.

Diane returned the next day and brought a cake, chocolate with white coconut icing. It was his father's favorite, and she sat on the floor and pushed spoon after spoon of it into his mouth until he began to move toward the spoon when she raised it. His lips could still not hold the food well and crumbs were on the edge of the couch and on the floor, but Wiley was amazed at the life struggling back into his father.

Wiley sat across the room in the old cane rocker and watched Diane, seeing her for the first time. Her long, straight dark hair moved sideways as she leaned her head to feed his father, like the tall reeds in a breeze, he thought.

Later that night, after she'd left, he went in the skiff to the camp, rowing down the dark channels through the tall saw grass. He felt as if he were rowing through her hair. Through her hair and into the last channel to the camp, the little shack, and the pen where the cat was. He lighted the lantern and hung it on the end post of the porch, going out to the edge of the light, to the pen, giving the cat the two possums he had trapped. The cat didn't seem to pay attention to the possums. Usually it didn't seem to notice the food he brought it, not until it thought it was alone. Then there would be a brief scuffle, and he would hear it in the dark, crunching the bones.

Time passed so quickly. His father recovered, and then he was gone. Diane didn't go with Wiley and the others to bury his father. It was too close to the time for her to have the baby, and her mother was there with her in the house, ready to help her when it came. The second stroke came quickly to his father. He was sitting at the table, finishing his dinner and talking about getting a TV so he could watch the news. He said it took too long to get the news by the papers and a TV was necessary. He knew from the neighbors that they could pick up at least one station from Miami, sometimes two. And a small black-and-white wouldn't cost much. "There's a lot to see these days," he said. He was finishing his coffee. His lips were in control, and he didn't have to worry about hot things anymore. Diane had nursed him back. Coffee was one of the things he loved most. He put down the empty cup. "There's a lot we're missing," he said. Then a strange look came into his eyes. Before Wiley could reach him from the other side of the table he slid onto the floor. The big hands lay open, with the fingers curled slightly up, as if he were holding them to receive the thing his eyes were staring toward.

The next week the November hurricane blew down the big palm, but it didn't harm either the camp or the pen where the cat was. A few pines were down in the woods, their trunks twisted and snapped off by the whirling winds. The cat lay still when Wiley went to feed it after the storm had blown over, and when he entered the cage he saw the cat was dead. He lifted its head in his hand. He couldn't tell what he was feeling. At first it seemed like a sickness inside him, down in his stomach, but then all the muscles in his body relaxed. He lay beside the cat's body and fell asleep.

Late in the afternoon he woke up. He lifted the cat and carried it to the skiff, stowed the shovel under the seat, and then pushed off. The channel toward the bay was full of trash from the storm, pine limbs and reeds and clumps of sea grass stirred up from the bottom by the waves. It was a long pull to Post Island.

He had it in mind to bury the cat at the foot of the palm. When he got to the island and saw that the hurricane had blown it down, he dug the hole anyway where he'd intended, about three feet long and two feet wide, down about four feet until he thought he was going to hit rock. But there was no rock. It struck him then why the tree grew so old there, a large deep depression in the marl. The sun was going down and he watched it out over the bay, thinking where he and Mack had been that night after the storm blew them across the water. He put the cat in the hole and said good-bye to it and filled the hole with sand. When he'd finished he sat on the crumbling stump of the palm and watched the sun turning flat as it went down into the water.

The week before, when they had buried his father, nothing had seemed finished the way he thought it should. He felt his father's life going on, like a debt he owed and couldn't repay. Now the cat was dead. But this time it was finished, all of it. He lay on the fallen trunk of the palm and looked at the water. He thought of his father lying those months on the couch, afraid to recover, but afraid he would not recover, too, and the cat in its pen, lying patiently until it thought it was alone. As if time didn't exist until it was alone.

He and Mack, lying together, side by side on the pier, both of them covered with mud like two swamp creatures, and then time starting up and Mack saying, "Hell, Wiley, that was the strangest fight I ever been in."

Then Wiley getting up and standing over Mack, looking into those eyes that stared up at him out of the mud, saying, "Me too," and wanting to say something else but not being able to. It was something like thank you, but it didn't make any sense to him. He stepped into the skiff and reached down for the cat. It hissed at him and arched its back, still lying there exhausted, but arching its back as if it would fight him to the death.

"Come on," he said to the cat. He folded one of the empty gunny sacks for the crabs and used it like a mitt to lift the cat carefully, holding it along its back so it couldn't bite or claw him. "You got a new life now," he said.

A Cabin in the Woods

Pickett was gone behind the rising wall of logs now, the only sign of him being the heavy grunts she heard as he tried to lift another one.

"You're going to bust a gusset," she yelled. She had no idea what a gusset was, but the warning had been her mother's favorite. Prinny hated it as a child but recently had begun to love rehearing her mother's voice. The saying brought forth an image of Pickett lying in a ward of the hospital, a busted gusset ward, rows and rows of plaintive faces waiting for their gussets to heal. Prinny could hear the high-pitched, scolding voice of her mother, hovering in a heaven of busted gussets. Her mother had warned her about marrying an older man like Pickett. She said he had creases at the base of his earlobes and would be old before his time. But here he was, about to turn forty, and still heaving logs that two normal men could barely lift.

It was already dark out in the swamp, and the spotlight glared from behind her where Pickett had attached it that morning to a spindly pine. He'd rigged a gas-powered generator, and that way they could have light whenever he came out to work on the cabin. Prinny didn't mind. Even if she was forced to watch her husband consume himself with madness long into the night, at least she

had the consolation of a good book. There was something reas-
suring about the motor purring behind her. It took the edge off
Pickett's grunts and curses.

The cabin was his obsession. His great-great-grandfather Earl
had been the last to live in it, before it was dismantled to make
way for the new Jones family home. The squared, rough-hewn
cypress logs had been stacked and stored for decades like a family
heirloom in a barn, while the family home thrived and then failed.
All that was left of the new house now was a root cellar full of rotted boards. The barn, too, had collapsed. Pickett had inherited the
whole mess a year ago and Prinny had gone the fifty-mile drive
with him into the Mississippi Delta to inspect it. When he'd first
told her he'd inherited the old family place from an obscure great-
uncle, she'd imagined a vast expanse of land, rolling pastures and
elegant magnolias, but everything had been sold off except a
couple of flat, worthless acres with a pesticide-polluted well and a
few decayed buildings leaning like the laziest of sentinels. Pickett
himself had been amazed. He hadn't seen the place in years. He
gawked with disbelief at how, in his lifetime, it had fallen so far.
The following week he hired a man with a bulldozer to come out
and clear off what was left of the collapsing farm buildings. It was
then that they had uncovered the logs of the old cabin.

Pickett had come home wild. "You won't believe it," he said,
slamming the front door so hard he shook the windows. "We found
the old cabin. Just like it was when I was a kid!" Prinny was in the
living room with Alfonso, their Persian cat, on her lap.

When Pickett came into the room, Alfonso jumped and ran.
His white fur vanished like a wispy ghost around the corner to the
kitchen. Pickett fell to his knees in front of the chair and grabbed
Prinny's knees, looking into her eyes. His face was like a saint's in
ecstasy.

"It's not even rotted. The timber's just like it was the day old Earl died in it."

"What cabin?" she said. The word conjured up mixed emotions for her. On the one hand she pictured the quaint, rustic cabin of Romantic poets. On the other was a little shack with pigs sprawled and flies buzzing the grease-soaked dirt floor.

"It was the cabin my great-great-grandfather died in. It used to be a slave cabin, and one of my relatives hid out there during the Civil War."

The Romantic poets were fleeing through the windows like scalded dogs.

"It was there when the dozer went through the old barn," he went on, hardly able to catch his breath. "All the logs were piled up nice and neat as you please."

"That's great, sweetie," she said, and she leaned over and gave him a kiss on the forehead. "Dinner's cold," she added. She got up and pulled him toward her by the arms. "I fixed a roast."

The lot in the woods had come later, like a natural outgrowth from the cabin, she thought, as if a long-buried virus had been dug up with its last victim and had renewed its ugly work. He bought the lot at a tax sale. She'd warned him that anything at a tax sale was worthless. If the previous owners knew enough about the land to stop paying taxes on it, then why should he know more than they did?

"They didn't have the cabin," he said, the resolution in his voice coming at her like a steel gate.

In those days, the cabin had taken on mythic proportions. Pickett remembered tales of General Grant visiting it on his way through Mississippi. He claimed even to have found the very log where Grant had stubbed out a cigar. The logs themselves were hewn from the cypress swamps by the Indians because Pickett's ancestor, "old great-great something" as Prinny began to think of him, had saved the life of some big-shot Indian in the forest.

Those Indian names. Pickett had gone to the old land grants and had found out the Indian who'd originally owned the tax-sale lot was named Icky-bat-foot, or something equally weird. The tax lot and the Jones family home were like the same place, Pickett told her. It was all a part of "the same vast fabric of history," he said, gloating over the way he and she were about to become part of it. Prinny looked at the old deed with its ornate handwriting in large loops and flourishes. There was something almost evil about its beauty. Old Icky had sold the land for a wagon load of blankets. Prinny imagined the Indians in the winter thinking what an enormous trick they'd played on the foolish whites, as they lay warm in their blankets while the well-dressed dupes were doubtless lying cold on the wet, icy ground of their 640 acres. 640 acres, what was that compared to blankets? A couple of words on a piece of paper.

Then Prinny looked down to the signatures. Icky's name had been written by someone else and below it was an X, described as his mark. Below that was another name and another X. Under it was written "her mark."

Her. Prinny felt another person like herself, a simple person making the only mark she would ever leave behind. Sitting in the lawn chair in the woods as the dark tightened around her, Prinny could feel the history, too, but not in the grand way Pickett saw it. The vast fabric of history was full of mosquitoes and gnats. The vast fabric of history was Pickett's moans and grunts and splinter-filled hands. The tax lot was a tiny knoll at the end of a long dirt road in the middle of a swamp. Once, there had been a woman who had signed her X and gone off with her husband and a wagon load of blankets into obscurity. That was the vast fabric of history.

"I'm eight months pregnant," she yelled over the wall. "I can't stand much more of this."

All that seemed to hear her were the dark pines whose rough-barked trunks rose from the forest floor like crusty centipede legs. Off in the swamp, some creature heaved up a deep thunking sound, over and over. It made her think of lying in the swamp, wet and smooth-skinned and blind, throwing out your voice to see if the world was still there. It was like the baby inside her, kicking its legs and turning. Then Pickett said, "You didn't have to come here. Why did you come?"

That stopped her. She didn't have an answer. She put down her novel, whose three bickering daughters were starting to bore her anyway. For the first time, it seemed, she looked closely at the cabin. Its front wall had risen to where its two windows and its door were enclosed. The windows were like eyes staring at her, and the door a large dark nose, as if Pickett were not building a cabin but a face that was slowly rising out of the swamp.

She had a silly thought. Maybe she came with Pickett because she was jealous. The cabin was another woman in his life. An old flat-faced thing with no personality who'd let him do whatever he wanted with her.

No, that was just too silly. Maybe she came with him because she was bored. Or maybe she was afraid something would happen to him, a log might fall, and he'd be without anyone to help. Nobody except his dead relative, old great-great somebody. She pictured the old troublemaker in his buckskins rescuing Indians right and left. Maybe he had cabins all over the countryside. What if the Indian he'd saved hadn't wanted to be rescued, what then? Would he have built the old busybody a cabin then? Or maybe the cabin was the Indian's way of revenge. Some sly self-destructive red man plotting against the offspring of his savior. Maybe he knew that once old great-great moved into the cabin his spirit would be trapped there. His and those of all his offspring, down to the thousandth generation. If you were a Jones, you were as good as dead. Cabin fever of the spirit. She wondered if the curse might apply to wives as well. Blankets and a wagon, make your X and then you're free.

"It's getting late," she said. "You're working yourself to death. Let's go home and eat."

He was muttering from behind the wall. "These goddamn logs," he said. "In the dark I can't tell which one's which anymore."

"Good then," she said, "it's time to go."

"Aha!" he said. "There you are." He sang out to Prinny, "Just one more and we'll call it a night."

Some kind of creature, an owl perhaps, let out a ghastly and complicated screech from high above them in the trees. Prinny was scared by the sound. For no reason she could discover, it made her think of the baby inside her. She felt an eerie kinship with the voice. It was like the voice of her mother if it had been transported into a bird. A gusset bird, that's what it was.

"Hurry up," she said to Pickett. "I don't like it out here in the dark."

"That was just an owl," he said. "Anyway, it's not my fault it's taking so long. If you weren't pregnant, you could be helping me. We'd be through by now."

She couldn't believe he'd finally said it. Not that she was shocked at the idea. She'd known all along he'd been thinking it. Behind the cabin he was heaving the log up against the wall, going on about his business as if he hadn't said a thing.

"So you finally got the guts to say it," she said calmly, more to herself than to him.

"Here goes!" he said. She saw the tip of the log swing up over the wall and slide forward. He was pushing each one up until it was balanced like a teeter-totter on the wall, and then he'd swing it around into place. He groaned loudly, and the log came to rest, balanced, wavering a little. She expected him to slide it around, but nothing happened.

The generator purred behind her. The empty eyes of the topless cabin stared at her from the center of its spotlight. "Pickett," she said. "Are you all right?" She heard a gasp of breath and jumped up from the lawn recliner. It was dark around the back of the cabin, and her eyes didn't adjust well. At first she thought he was stretched out facedown at her feet, but that was only a log. Then she saw him a few feet farther, curled on his side. "Oh, Pickett," she said.

He was still gasping, but his breath was coming back to him. "I pulled something," he said.

In the hospital, their regular doctor, Dr. Geiger, was too busy flirting with a chipmunk-faced, short-legged nurse to tell Prinny what the story was on Pickett. Then she saw the surgeon down the hall, and she cornered him near the elevator. He was a big man with high cheekbones and a dark tan. She was opening her mouth to ask him about Pickett, when she realized he looked like an Indian, and her heart froze. His black eyes glared down at her. "Is there something I can do for you?" he said.

Her head was swimming. All she could think of to say were Pickett's words, "the vast fabric of history." Then a sharp pain hit her hard in the stomach.

When she came to, she was in a bed and Pickett was standing beside her. She had another pain, and she realized the contractions had started. The baby was coming. It was weeks early, but it was coming. The room was full of light, too much light, and Pickett's blue shirt shone like the surface of a deep, clear lake.

"Are you all right?" he said. He was wearing his kind face, the one that made him seem years younger than he was.

"Me?" she said weakly. "What about you?"

He was standing stiffly, and she knew he was in pain. "I'm OK," he said. "The surgeon said it wasn't a hernia, thank goodness. It's just a pulled ligament. But it hurts like hell." He bent over and stroked her forehead with his palm. "So we're going to be parents at last," he said. "After all these years."

"You sound happy about it again."

"I was always happy."

"Even when I couldn't help you with the cabin?"

"I'm sorry," he said. "It got away from me. I wanted to finish it before you had the baby. I wanted you to be able to have the baby in the cabin."

"What?"

"Just like in the old days," he said. His eyes were simple and bright. She wanted to lash out at him, to say, "What kind of lame-brained idiocy is that?" But as she looked into his face, its innocence overcame her. She was stunned.

"You're a child, Pickett," she said. And there he was, beneath the short-trimmed graying beard and the forehead already turning to wrinkles, not the man old before his time whom her mother had warned her about, but a child.

Parents. They were going to be parents together after all. Why hadn't he ever said he wanted her to have the baby in the cabin?

She knew it was because he had wanted to surprise her with the idea. If he'd said it earlier, she would have called him a fool, right then and there. Then, she remembered her junior year in college when they'd first fallen in love and had gone to France for the summer together. She remembered the little French village on the Marne where they'd stayed, and how on the chimney of the house next door a stork was building its giant nest. They had watched it through the window of their room and the whole scene had seemed so romantic, the stork gliding to its precarious perch and weaving its unbelievable nest of awkward sticks against the backdrop of the orange-tiled roofs and the tall spire of the cathedral and the rolling hills. Pickett was like that stork, his gangly, stooping body lifting the huge branches and carrying them to an impossible place.

She had another contraction, this one stronger, and it took her awhile to catch her breath. When her head cleared, he was still there with his palm stroking her forehead and his simple face. Drawn to that face she had soared into it, the vast fabric of history, like a maiden with her wide skirts spread.

Later, between the contractions, the doctor came in and told her the baby was turned wrong, and they'd need to do a Caesarean. His face was surrounded by a white light with rainbows at the edges. The nurses crowded in, and one gave Prinny a shot just before they lifted her to the gurney. Pickett walked beside her down the hallway and held her hand.

Maybe it would have been easier in a cabin, she thought. There wouldn't have been anywhere to roll her, and now she didn't want to be rolled anywhere at all. Her stomach churned. Then, that passed and she was peaceful. They stopped at the door to the operating room, and Pickett's face loomed down at her, surrounded by the same white glow and rainbows as the doctor's had been. It wasn't so much his face as it was the cabin's, out in the woods in its spotlight. She wasn't herself anymore either, she was the woman who had signed her X and left with her wagon full of blankets. She was the female stork whose mate had made her a nest that was beautiful and impossible. I would have died if I hadn't left, she thought.

She tried to focus on Pickett, but his face was just a fuzz in the whiteness. "Having the baby in the cabin would have been nice," she said. It was easy to say now. She had signed her X, and she was free. She pulled the crisp sheet up to her neck. Safe. She smiled and placed her sweating hands over his.

Out from Guadalajara

Chapell had never known there was any etiquette to traveling on buses, especially in Mexico, where it seemed that everyone pushed on board as quickly as possible and you grabbed whatever seat you could. This was going to be a long ride, to Morelia, then to Pátzcuaro. He'd heard about the little colonial town near a lake in the mountains from the girl he met on the ferry coming across from La Paz to Los Mochis.

It was going to be a long ride, so he was glad when he found the counter for an express bus and they gave him a reserved seat. He did not speak any Spanish, and it had been difficult to get across to the old man at the counter that he didn't want the slow bus. Then he didn't know how to ask which bay the bus was located in. "Where?" he said, and the old man, whose face was round and punctuated with quick, dark eyes like a bird's, pointed to the door. "No, the bus," Chapell slowly drew with his finger a couple of imaginary parking spaces on the counter and said, "Number, which number?"

The old man smiled and said something very rapidly. Chapell stared at him. Then a younger man who'd been helping another person rushed over and wrote two numbers, 36–37, on a scrap of paper and shoved it at Chapell without saying a word. "Thanks," Chapell said.

When he got to the loading area and found the bus in the loading dock with the right number, it wasn't an express bus at all. It was just another Flecha Amarilla, like all the others that stopped at every town, every wayside, every cluster of people, or couple of people, or single person alone in the middle of nowhere. Just over the rise of a hill the bus screeches to a halt and the *campesino* tracks his dusty way down the aisle, while Chapell, thinking, always thinking, knows that a truck is rushing madly over the hill behind them, unable to stop.

He walked up to the bus in the terminal, trying to ignore a group of small children yelling, *"chicle, chicle,"* who with their trays of gum had trailed him from inside like a school of minnows nibbling at a diseased fish. He had learned that you didn't stand around and you didn't wait for the driver or his assistant, the ticket taker, to open the luggage compartment under the bus. You went back there yourself, and if it wasn't one of those that required a long L-shaped hex key to open it, you opened the compartment and threw in your bags. You threw them in with the crates of cabbage and god-knows-what, the cans of oil, the grimy pieces of bus engine that usually found their way there.

He stowed his suitcase in the least oily spot and then stepped on board. The trip was a long one, so he'd brought in his knapsack an avocado, a package of saltines, and a jar of strange-looking peanut butter he'd found in a market, which appeared to have swirls of chocolate in it. At least he hoped it was chocolate.

He had not come prepared for his trip through Mexico. Neglecting even to get a Spanish phrase book, he'd gone over to his mother's house one afternoon and handed her his pet hamster at the door. "I'm going to Mexico," he said.

She had looked at him with her eyebrows furrowed but took the hamster, shaking its cage and peering into the hollowed-out duck decoy, full of cedar shavings, that was its lair. "It's in there, isn't it?" she said. Then, without waiting for an answer, she said: "What's in Mexico?"

He hadn't been able to tell her. Nor could he tell his father whom he'd called earlier on the phone. His father, in his casual way of expecting the worst, had said: "I trust you'll keep an eye out for hepatitis?"

He hadn't seen his father in the three months since his parents' divorce became final. It was too much for him to see the sad but resigned way his father accepted his mother's decision to "lead her own life." Ever since he was fifteen and had started to think about such things, he had not been able to understand his father's odd practicality. Did expecting the worst prepare you for it? How did one prepare for hepatitis? Still, on the phone with his father describing how ten years ago a neighbor's son had gone to Mexico and had come back on a stretcher, his face an orange-yellow, Chapell found himself agreeing. The neighbor's son was suspected of having caught the disease from shooting drugs, but that didn't seem to make a difference.

So far he had done well. He'd made it all the way down the Baja Peninsula, across on the ferry, and inland to Guadalajara, with the only two words of Spanish he knew—*cuanto* and *quiero*—how much and I want. Of course he'd learned other words, the words for food, by ordering from menus and seeing what came, but those words he couldn't count because he never said them without looking at a menu first.

The seat number on his ticket was 39, near the back of the bus, a window seat. He went to it and found his place already occupied by an old man who appeared very sick. The white-haired woman next to him, her shoulders wrapped in a black rebozo, was rubbing his forehead with a cloth, the sweat coming up in new full beads almost as soon as she wiped it.

Chapell wanted to tell the old man he was in the wrong seat, but he knew that without any Spanish he would only make a fool of himself trying. He sat down in the seat across from them and began to eat his food. I hope it's not catching, he thought, as he watched the man, who appeared to have passed out, his mouth lolling open and his head rocking from side to side as the bus pulled out of the station.

The girl, Randi, had said he didn't have any character, that was what came out after she'd twisted up her mouth and spit her gum on the sidewalk when she left him. He didn't want to remember the rest of her face now, but the mouth he couldn't help seeing. They'd met on the ferry and had gone to Yelapa together, spending a week in a little shack near the beach. "What do you expect?" he'd said back to her. "What does a chubby little airhead like you expect?"

The bus was getting to the edge of Guadalajara, and a man carrying an automobile muffler, who had waved down the bus a couple of blocks from the station, got off. The bus churned out from the roadside and slung the sick man's head against the window with a dull thunk. The old woman tried to prop his head back up.

But she wasn't an airhead and she knew it. Why hadn't he said anything else? That was what scared him. He should have showed her. Showed her what? Slapped her? Wasn't that what people with character were supposed to do? Like somebody tough in a movie who didn't take crap from anybody, and if you gave them any crap they slapped you around so you'd respect them. He imagined his father slapping his mother, trying to slap some sense into her. His father would never do anything like that, and Chapell knew that he wouldn't either. You couldn't slap someone into loving you.

As the highway straightened into the countryside, there was a dead horse on the side of the road and he watched it go by the window, as if on a conveyor belt, its belly swollen and its legs stiff. The pavement underneath it was stained dark from the fluids draining from the horse. Damn, he thought, don't they have any respect down here? It was not the first dead horse he'd seen. When he was with the girl, after they had come up from the coast and had first traveled into the mountains a few miles outside of Tepic, they'd seen another horse, already shrunken to bones and skin.

"How can they do that?" she'd said.

"Do what?"

"Let a horse rot on the side of the road."

"They don't care, I guess." He didn't want to talk about it. Only one thing depressed him more than death and that was not caring about anything. Sometimes he thought about it, coming into his life like a disease, but without pain, a slow progression until everything else seemed distant, as if he were floating on a raft and the shore was drifting farther away.

He remembered her mouth again, and the gum, the way it landed on the pavement with a small bubbly pool of clear spittle around it. She'd smiled when he called her an airhead.

"You don't even have enough character to fall in love. You never will," she said.

He had thought about falling in love with her. And one day when he saw her out on the beach and she'd just come in from the waves, he thought about her cutoff jean shorts, the way her stomach was flabby but still sexy with her firm breasts coming out above it. Love, he thought, was something that made you turn over inside. And you thought about it a lot. And that was what he'd started to do since he had been with her. He thought about it a lot after he had first made love with her in the sweaty darkness of the little hut. He listened to her breathing. He'd never seen anyone put so much of herself into love. She caught it deep down in her throat, like love was down there coming up out of her stomach.

"I love you," he said finally in the darkness after the fourth night they'd made love.

Her breathing stopped. She turned onto her side toward him. Her long straight blond hair hung across her neck and caught the moonlight through the doorway. Under the mosquito netting, he felt as if they were in a tent, hidden from the world, even though there was no door in the hut and anyone could have walked in and seen them there together naked under the netting. Hidden. Maybe that was what love was, he thought. A feeling like being hidden together with someone.

She was looking into his face, but she didn't say anything. Then she turned back over and went to sleep.

Or maybe not caring was only a symptom. You couldn't prevent what was going to happen, but, like his father, you needed to know you'd watched for it. A divorce, a dead horse on the side of the road, falling in and out of love. He was on the raft, drifting, but how had he gotten here? How did one come to the point where he no longer cared?

At first the sick man had been moaning, so softly that Chapell could barely hear it. The sound was more like something that he sensed without knowing exactly where it was coming from, like a deep, slow vibration, a part of the bus itself and its motion over the highway as it rocked through the green hills and into the rich cropland valleys that lay to the east of Guadalajara. As the afternoon wore on, the moaning became imperceptible, if it still existed at all. The man's sleep was quiet, and where his forehead had at first been covered with oily sweat, it was smooth and dry. The old woman had fallen asleep also and Chapell stared at them for a long while, wondering what they were like. He noticed that in her left hand, which was dark and leathery on the back, but lighter and stretched smooth in its palm, she held loosely a small strand of beads with a cross attached and on it a dark red wooden Jesus. Her clothes looked as if they had been worn steadily for years, washed a thousand times until the fabric, although it had no holes in it, was worn down and the colors faded. Then he noticed her shoes. She'd taken them off and they lay on their sides by her feet, two black shoes that looked as if they'd never been worn. Had she bought them in Guadalajara? Or maybe, he thought, they were shoes that she wore only when she went to the city. And only sickness, the need for a doctor, would bring her to the city.

Randi hadn't worn any shoes either. The whole time they were in Yelapa, she hadn't worn any. "What if you cut your foot and it gets infected?" he'd said. She told him to mind his own business. For some strange reason he was glad when she said it. For a moment he'd been hurt and mad, and then suddenly he was happy. He wanted to tell her he was happy. He was standing outside the hut and smiling at her while she leaned over beside the bed. She'd just come in from the ocean and was removing her wet shorts. Then he watched as she stood with nothing on, wringing the water out of them. But he couldn't say anything. He just stood there and watched her until she noticed him.

"Quit watching me," she said.

"Sorry," he said. He walked off toward the row of trees that separated the hut from the beach. He sat down beside one and leaned his back against its trunk. Here I am, he thought. Here I am in paradise.

Remembering, and looking out of the bus as it wound into the red dirt mountains of Michoacán, he realized the odd thing was that there had been nothing sarcastic or cynical about the thought. At the time, it seemed that the more difficult she was, the more he thought he loved her.

"You can think," she said standing on the sidewalk in Guadalajara, nudging the spittle and the gum with her right big toe. "But that's as far as you can go." She'd turned then and walked from him, the duffel bag containing all her things slung over her shoulder like a giant, navy blue sausage.

"And you can go rot in hell," he said. He had surprised himself, thinking with such violence and saying that to her. If it had been in his power to send her into the flames of hell he would have done it gladly. The violence of his feeling frightened him and at the same time strangely pleased him. Randi turned for a moment, and the duffel bag swung around, almost tipping her off balance. She looked at him, as if she were thinking, as if she were about to change her mind and walk back to him. He could hear her saying it, "I'm sorry," and then he would forgive her.

But she said nothing, and after she'd stared at him for what seemed like at least a minute, she turned and continued down the street away from him.

It was beginning to grow dark in the valleys between the mountains to the east and the bus driver was no longer stopping to pick up as many passengers, so they were making better time. Still, it would be at least three more hours to Pátzcuaro and that irritated Chapell. He hated searching for a room later in the night when they knew you were desperate. Suddenly he felt envious of all the others on the bus. They had homes to go to, food waiting for them when they got there. He was getting hungry, and all his food was gone.

He looked over at the old woman and the sick man. They hadn't eaten anything all day. They're probably used to it, he thought.

The woman was asleep and so was the man, his jaw hanging down and his cheeks sunken in. The two of them were so peaceful, like a pair of figurines, the kind Chapell's grandmother used to collect and put in a cabinet in the dining room, people and animals and little creatures that were neither wholly animals nor wholly people, which frightened him until his mother made up stories about them to explain how they got that way. What kind of life did the old people have? Were they in love? Chapell had almost been afraid to look at them earlier. Still, something was drawing him toward them. He wasn't sure what it was, but when he looked at them he felt it was the way they belonged together. He couldn't explain it. The closest thing he could think of was his grandmother and her house, the old house his mother had grown up in. There was no separating her from it. Once when she came to visit them at Christmas, Chapell noticed how strange she was away from the house. And yet, it seemed that the house had come with her, as if their own house were no longer quite the same. As she moved through it, the rooms were gradually changing, becoming more and more the old house, her house, the house that his mother had been born in. He could even smell it, a smell like dry old wood, the wood of rafters in the attic.

Watching the old couple asleep, he tried to think of Randi again, to place her beside him the way the old woman was beside the sleeping old man. He imagined himself across the aisle, dreaming of their life together, but it wouldn't work. He knew it was all in his head and he would never be like the old man. What would he dream? He had never been sick, not as sick as the old man, and he'd never had anyone love him. His dreams would be empty thoughts.

He looked over at the old man and realized that the man's eyes were half open. Was he sleeping with his eyes open? Chapell leaned forward a little to get a better look. Even in the twilight, from the last bit of sun that was coming in from the old man's side through the window, Chapell could tell he was dead. As soon as he realized it, the breath went out of him and he struggled to get his wind.

The woman's eyes opened suddenly. She looked directly at him. She was wide awake, and he knew she had never been asleep.

She whispered something.

He didn't know how to answer. She must have realized he knew about the old man and he saw that it frightened her for him to know. She didn't say anything, but she was looking at him with her eyes wide and anxious, shaking her head back and forth. No, no, she seemed to be telling him.

He shrugged and looked away from her to the front of the bus. She must have gone crazy, he thought. She must have lost it when the old man died. I've got to try to tell the driver, he thought. Somebody's got to do something about this.

Suddenly her arm was across the aisle, and her hand was wiry and hard around his wrist, and she was hissing at him. Not loud, a low hiss under her breath. No words, but there was an intensity in her black eyes, even in the falling darkness.

She was holding him in his seat, holding him desperately. For a moment he struggled, trying to wrench his arm free, but then he was no longer afraid, as if something in her had come out of her hand into his body, calming him, making him relax and sit back in his seat. She let his wrist go and she smiled at him, a sweet smile, which he could not understand.

Then he was no longer thinking. He felt something, as if his mother had come into the room when he was a child and was sick. She didn't have to ask him what he wanted, and he didn't have to tell her. Along the edges of his heart there was a feeling. He didn't understand it. There were no words for it.

Then he understood everything. The old woman and her husband were two of the poor ones who lived out away from the towns. They were the people whom Chapell had cursed, the ones who stood along the road and made the bus stop for them.

If he told the bus driver the old man was dead, then there would have to be an investigation. When they got to the next town, the authorities would haul the old man's body off the bus. And then what would she do? Miles from their home, from anyone to help her?

He looked over at her, and she was still smiling. She was looking into his eyes and it embarrassed him. In that moment of embarrassment, Randi came back to him, like a vision, there in the night in the hut, her straight blond hair hanging across her neck, and standing beside the bed wringing out her shorts, and shoving her toe into the spittle around the lump of gum on the sidewalk in Guadalajara. He couldn't remember her face. He could not remember. Then he came out of his thoughts. The thing he couldn't understand, the woman's smile, was still before him.

The embarrassment dropped from his body like a rush of cold water. In its place was an understanding between them, he and the old woman. When she saw it she turned from him and put her face into the shoulder of the dead man, weeping quietly.

There were no other passengers in the few rows directly in front of them and so no one could hear the old woman weeping. When they pulled into the brightly lit terminal in Morelia, she managed to be quiet for a while and sat up in her seat. A young couple got on and sat down a couple of rows up but they began whispering in each other's ears and didn't seem to notice anyone else. After the bus pulled out and reached the darkness of the countryside, the old woman began again. Her weeping was almost like breathing, regular and relaxed. Once, the girl leaned into the aisle and looked back as if she'd heard, but Chapell coughed and started clearing his throat. The girl smiled at him and turned back to her boyfriend.

They were in the mountains again, and Chapell saw in the light from the half-moon that beside the road were large trees without much underbrush between them. There had been no towns to speak of, only a few clusters of adobe houses here and there off the side of the road. The bus passed around the edge of a lake that looked man-made, its dirt shoreline hundreds of feet wide where the water level had gone down. What remained of the lake looked in the moonlight like a toy metal plate dropped into the lap of a girl's light brown dress.

Chapell was reminded of his mother. The little, blue doll's tea set she kept from when she was a child. He could still see her putting it into a brown cardboard box on the bed, wrapping the pieces carefully. He'd given up wondering about the divorce. He'd realized that both his parents were stronger than he was. Like two stone statues on the shore of an island, in the distance they were lifelike, standing together, greeting him. Closer, he saw how enormous they were, farther and farther apart the closer he moved toward them. He could no longer feel any sadness about them.

As the bus rounded the lake, the water appeared to turn under the strip of light from the moon. The old woman sat up and looked out the window. Then she nodded to Chapell. Yes, yes it's time. He got up and moved across the aisle to help her with the old man. The bus was swinging around the curves going down the side of the mountain and it was tough getting at the old man. In his mind earlier Chapell had thought only of the weight of the old man, imagining that he would be limp like a drunk. But the old man was stiff.

Luckily he'd had his legs out straight when he died, so that even though it was difficult to get him out of the seat, once they had him out, he didn't look all that strange, only bent a little at the waist and at the knees. As Chapell pulled him out and into the aisle, holding him around the chest, he caught an odd smell, like some kind of medicine. The old woman helped him, and they made their way to the front of the bus.

The old woman had timed it perfectly. As they reached the front she told the bus driver to stop, and she and Chapell carried the old man between them down the steps and onto the ground below. The bus driver seemed suspicious, but Chapell was between him and the old man so the driver couldn't get a good look.

"*Borracho?*" the driver said, tipping up his hand like a man drinking as they went down the steps.

"*Si, si,*" the woman said. "*Borracho.*"

A dirt road led off up the side of a gap between two hills. Chapell could just make out in the darkness a group of houses packed close together where the road disappeared around the side of the hill on the right. There were only a couple of lights. It looked so lonely, the dim yellow lights in the vast darkness of the mountains.

Along the highway was a low stone wall and they took the old man there, lowering him to the ground and leaning his head and shoulders awkwardly against the crumbling rocks. The bus driver revved up the engine.

Chapell wanted to say something. To tell the old woman how he felt. The night was cool and he smelled the diesel exhaust faintly in the cool air, almost sweet, like a perfume. At first, he thought he wanted to tell her he was sorry her husband had died, but that wasn't it. They'd loved each other. Nothing he could tell her would add to that. It was really something about himself that he wanted to say, but there were no words for it. He looked down at the dead man and saw how white and dead he was in the cold air of the mountains.

He leaned over and put his hands on the old woman's shoulders and felt her thin bony body under the rebozo. She reached up with her right arm and the tips of her fingers touched him on the cheek, her hand shaking a little and her callused skin rough as it wavered against him. They both looked down. Then he ran, ran to the bus and leaped up, high on the steps.

Sea Dogs

Think of us as boys, the kind who like to flake off rust wherever they see it. Imagine we're at work on your car at night in the parking lot, up underneath with wide-bladed screwdrivers, like snakes escaping the flood. Or maybe in the dry bathtub while you're at work. We get down on our knees and dig at the drain. We chip a little pile of pieces and put them carefully into plastic baby bottles, which we keep on shelves in the galley of our ship. We watch with satisfaction while the bottles fill, the rust like a red-brown rum, aging, mellowing, waiting for some moment of need. Treasure.

Maybe it comforts you that the high seas and the romantic past are the only places you'll run into us, as if we're no more than pages in a book. Think again. We're no dream. I, Morales, am the king of the pirates. I am at your doorstep.

My mother is a small woman. She lived in a village. I say this to soothe your mind, because I know that you don't want to hear how I was born in your city, under a streetlamp, while a cab driver complained and my mother sobbed and screamed. You don't give a damn that I grew up stealing hubcaps and radios. I'm the kind that belongs in jail.

But this is where I've fooled you. This is where I tell you how

I spent my hours hiding in the library. I read and read and read. About the pirates. They had no fathers. They rose up from the rotting decks of ships, like vapors escaping from the hold. The code of the pirate is to take all the prisoners he can. Even if they're no good for ransom he can always bring them over, make them into his own kind. When you see us at the bus stop, with our bandanas wrapped around our heads and the glint of blades between our teeth, think of us as missionaries. We've come to convert you.

Outside my house this morning I found on the sidewalk by the gate a dried puddle of blood and two wavering trails of spattered drops going in opposite directions down the street. I record these things in my log. When you're finding your way on the open sea, any clue can save you. The bird flying against the wind with a brown twig in its mouth, the piece of red driftwood, the evening sky that flattens the sun.

A pirate has a simple life. We love the night. The stars above guide our way. The rush of the waves against the bow is like the sound of cars on the wet street. The stealing, the ransom, the mayhem, those are just excuses to be on the open sea. We long to catch the glimmer of a distant ship, to make the whispered rounds waking our mates for battle. Along alleyways, by garbage cans, we watch the deep brick sides of buildings with their windows lighted far too late like moons, and we imagine you inside.

My girlfriend doesn't think much of this. She says I can be a real jerk. That's not as strong as her language gets. So you can see how I need two lives. The one in port, the one at sea. Her name is Ellis, and she's taller than I am. She says I'm really an intellectual at heart and I have no business fooling around with such a crowd. I tell her she's my Malinché, the Indian who was the mistress of Cortés. He was a pirate, too, but he was smart and wrote letters to the king to make sure everything went right. Malinché was his interpreter and his lover. There's no telling what she told the Indians, how she changed what Cortés said. She didn't say what he wanted her to say, she said what she knew would make him a prince. No book says that, but I know it. It worked, and he fooled Montezuma and all of them. He took a couple of hundred guys and beat an army of hundreds of thousands. That's the way pirates are.

The girlfriend of a pirate should have a secret beauty that no one understands. She should be difficult and passionate. No one can trust her except the pirate, and even then she does things that he thinks are all wrong. He only learns later about the secret intrigue, how she was stabbing him in the back in order to save his life.

Ellis could be like that, but she doesn't cooperate. She says what I want her to say when we're with other people. It's only when we're alone that she says the good things that surprise me and make me feel foolish. Ellis is a spoiled rich girl from Queens College. She saw at once that I was a pirate.

Even a pirate has to have a day job. I work inside the Statue of Liberty and rescue the ones who panic halfway up the tight spiral stairs. You know how it is, lockstep, with one person's knees in your face and another right behind you sucking at your heels. The clang of shoes on the steel footings, each step a dungeon door slamming shut, an endless stream of people taking the final walk. Liberty, my ass. They get up about fifty feet, and they feel the air get tight. Their hearts start to pound. They're on the edge of the pirate's plank with their hands tied behind them, and the ship is rocking, and below is the clear blue water of the sea that's like air and goes down forever. They imagine themselves dropping over the side, holding their breaths, and the pressure getting heavier and heavier until they finally have to take it in.

That's when the whimper gets louder. The fingers clutch the

rail. The lungs draw deep. They try to sit down, but there's nowhere to do it. If they had any sense they'd step off the edge and get it over with. But they hang there, inside the Statue of Liberty, on the open sea, and the whimper turns to a whine and then a scream.

Ellis . . . every day on my way to work I pass the island named for her and think of all the poor slobs who came through there. Their ghosts, like the whispering sirens, call me. The huddled masses. But pirates don't come from anywhere and they don't have any past. They never sign a name. They cut through the huddled masses like a dagger through wax. They sail away and smile through blood.

A few months ago, Ellis called me over to her apartment. "Isn't it time we did something more permanent?" she said. She sat next to me on the couch and rubbed my temples, the way I like it, with her thumbs moving real slow and sliding across my skin.

"What do you mean?" I said.

"I mean like move in together, like marriage."

I tried to get out of the grip of her thumbs but she pressed harder, pushing up. My head was coming off. The pirate's head, severed and bloody, raised to the parapet for the whole town to see. "Arrgh! I don't know," I said. "My mother. . . ."

"Your mother doesn't need you living there with her anymore. It's been five years since your father died. And you live upstairs anyway. You hardly ever see her." Ellis's face was innocent, the innocent betrayer. Dark curly hair tied back in a knot, a white lace frill around the collar.

Sometimes pirates have mothers. It's one of those things you don't expect, but there it is. They're the pirate's cross, the burden to bear, the long chain that trails from every ship and reaches back to port.

"She still needs me," I said.

"I need you," she said. She let her thumbs drop. My head floated before it sank back onto my neck.

"She'll cry," I said.

Ellis looked at me. She was all black robes and the white dusted hair of the magistrate. "Your mother's a goddamn bartender and carries a piece," she said. "Don't give me that song and dance."

"I need to go to the bathroom," I said.

"Oh, Mory," she said, "don't run away. Can't we talk about this?"

I got up and went into the bathroom and closed the door. I needed the quiet. When you're in a bathroom you can be anywhere. On a ship in the South Seas. Becalmed in a harbor. Waiting for the slap of oars as the crew comes back from shore.

It's time to count your treasure.

Ellis, Ellis, Ellis, Ellis. Sometimes I say her name over and over when I'm about to go to sleep. It's the leaves of palm trees rustling in the breeze. The shift of grass skirts.

She had calmed down when I came out of the bathroom. Like the water lapping the shore after a storm. Fresh air. The cool breeze. She had fixed some tea. She smiled at me, and we sat on the couch drinking it in silence. Finally, when we had finished, she took my hand in hers.

"That job is rough on you, isn't it, sweetie?" she said. I appreciated that she wasn't getting on my case for going into the bathroom.

"It's not so bad," I said.

"Cooped up all day in that statue with all those tourists. I couldn't stand it."

"I feel important," I said. "People need me."

"I need you," she said. She kissed my neck and undid the top button of my shirt and pulled one side down over my shoulder. Her warm breath swept across my chest, and she began kissing me there. "You're crazy," she said, "and a horrible liar. But I love you."

Working in the Statute of Liberty is like working inside your worst dream. It's all framework and dim light and people moving. It's the sounds of their feet and their coughs. From the bottom, you can't see the ones near the top, only the ones who are just starting up or coming back down. The sound of their shoes on the spiraling metal steps is the march of prisoners on the long last walk.

"It's the double helix of life," my friend Sturgis said one night after we'd left work and shared a couple of bottles of wine, sitting in a little park down near Wall Street. Sturgis is my first mate, the dreamer. His only treasure is stars in the sky.

"Give me another drink," I said.

"Ain't no more," he said. He placed the last bottle carefully by his feet. "The double helix makes us what we are," he said.

"Yo ho ho and a bottle of helix," I said.

"Treasure," he said.

"Arrgh! Make 'em walk the plank," I said.

We went back to his van, and thirty minutes later we were behind the building we'd been keeping our eyes on. The superintendent was off on Thursdays. 11.45 P.M. The tides were right. There she stood, tall and proud, all eleven stories of her, sailing in the night air. We jimmied the outside door to the basement.

Down the steps, her hold was dark and damp. A few rats scurried in the corners. Sturgis lit the oil lamp and the dim outlines of her cargo swam into view. The copper pipes hung across the ceiling like bars of tarnished brass. The big iron ones were wrapped in white like bandaged arms. The gray circuit boxes on the walls were chests ready to be opened. The silver tombs of the boilers with all their dials and gauges waited to be plucked like jewels.

I sent my mate to cut the main lines while I went to work on the first boiler, the gauges, the knobs, the breakers. Behind me Sturgis's hacksaw rasped across the copper pipes. I put the gems into my sack and went for the main circuit panel. I skipped the big 200-amp breakers and went for the thirties and twenties first. What I love is to work them in and out a couple of times before scuttling them. I imagine the old folks half asleep upstairs watching Leno. Then the deadly first blinks . . . off, on, off. How long will it be this time? they wonder. Is she going down for good?

Sturgis is more methodical than I am. He works his arm back and forth with the saw, getting into a rhythm that makes me want to lie on the deck and feel the ship sway beneath me. You were someone else's, my love, and now you're mine. Sturgis knows an artist in SoHo who buys all the pipe and the other things we decide not to keep. But for me it's not the money. Every building is a ship on the open sea.

I swung the booty over my shoulder and helped Sturgis gather the pipes. Once you scuttle her, you have to get out quick. When we walked up the stairs, a man was standing in the light of the door. He motioned us out with a pistol.

"These waters mine," he said, like he'd been reading the same books I had. He had a thick accent, a mix of things I couldn't place. He was about sixty, with bushy eyebrows and gray knots of hair over his ears. He might have been from Eastern Europe. A big scar snaked across his left cheek and his hands shook. Sturgis was edgy. As we came up the stairs and out into the open lot behind the building, I could tell he was looking for a chance to jump the old man.

"What do you want?" I said. "Do you live here?"

"I live there," he said. Without ever turning his eyes, he pointed to an empty building. There were holes in the tops of his shoes.

"We don't want no trouble," Sturgis said. "My uncle works in this building. He sent us down to get some old scrap in the basement."

The old man didn't pay any attention to Sturgis. He was looking straight at me.

"What flag are you flying?" I said.

He smiled. The gun dropped a little. "You carry all that to my place," he said. "Then I decide what to do."

If I hadn't seen the gun drop when I said that about the flag, I wouldn't have taken one step. Something told me it would be OK if I could keep talking.

"Come on, Sturgis," I said.

One thing about Sturgis. He'll take directions. He and I walked ahead with the things we'd stolen, and the old man followed us. When we were halfway across the empty lot between the two buildings, he started to talk.

"Name's Gregory," he said. "Here for ten years. Now you come in."

"You can ring up my uncle," Sturgis said. "He'll vouch for us." Sturgis was an idealist but he was a liar, too. His lies were always filled with words he never used. *Vouch.* As if anybody in Sturgis's family had ever *vouched* for anything.

Gregory lived in the basement of the nearby building. Somehow, he had run power into it even though it was abandoned. We went down a narrow stairway, and he told Sturgis to set the pipes along the wall at the bottom. Then he motioned me through the door into the place where he'd been living. The light was out when we came in, but all around us on the walls were what looked like big round eyes gleaming in the dim reflection from the stairway. The old man flipped a switch. It was a big room with boards as paneling to cover the cement walls. Hanging on the walls were hundreds of dials and gauges, every kind you could think of.

"Set the bag down," he said to me.

"Oh, man!" Sturgis said, gawking at the walls. "Man, oh man, oh man." He walked around staring at the gauges.

The old man smiled when Sturgis said it, but I could tell he didn't like Sturgis being over there.

"You sit down," he said. "We talking."

We sat in chairs at a round kitchen table in the center of the room. The place was fixed up pretty nice, with a little stove and refrigerator in one corner, and throw rugs here and there. There was no bed, but a hammock hung from the ceiling near the stove.

"Mr. Gregory," I said, "We don't want to take up your time. We can just leave what we took here with you and go on our way."

Gregory reached under the table and opened a wooden box and took out a bottle of cheap rum. He uncapped it, took a swig, and passed it to Sturgis. Then he proceeded to tell us his life story. Poor old salt, I thought. He'd been waiting for ten years for somebody to come along. We passed the bottle, and the story progressed. Sure enough, he'd been at sea, from the time he ran away at fifteen until he was fifty. He never told us where he was from, but he must have told us every place he'd ever been: Perth and Cartagena and Valparaiso, the Seychelles and McMurdo Sound, Calcutta, Cape Horn, and the Bering Strait. He was on Aden when we finished the first bottle, and he opened another.

By the time we'd finished the second bottle he was speaking English about a third of the time. The rest of it sounded like five or six languages stirred up. He turned back and forth from me to Sturgis. His eyes were dilated and full of fire. He drained the last drops from the bottle and reached under the table, but came up empty.

"Dead men tell no tales," he said.

"You sound just like my father," I said. Never mind that I'd never met my father. After that, he got sloppy, and Sturgis clouted him on the head with one of the bottles. I picked up the gun and saw that it wasn't even loaded. We collected our things and were heading out the door when I looked back at him. He wasn't dead, but he was bleeding from the scalp and was laid out on the floor by the table.

I couldn't leave him. The ship was burning, and he was the only one left on board.

"Come back," I said to Sturgis. He was already halfway up the steps. "Let's get the old man. We can take him to my mother's house."

Staring down at me from above, Sturgis had the copper pipes bundled under his arms. He looked like a huge ape carrying flagpoles. "Have you lost your freaking lid?" he said. "That old lush wanted to kill our asses."

"The gun wasn't loaded," I said.

"He probably didn't know that!"

"Come on," I said. "He's just like us."

We took the pipes and the bag with the gauges to the van and went back for the old man. He was sunk into his baggy clothes and was lighter than he looked. We put him in the back of the van, trying to make him comfortable. On the way uptown he started to come to, but then we heard him snoring and knew he'd be no trouble.

"He tells me about his travels," my mother said, and her eyes shone.

I'll never know why I decided to take Gregory to my house that night, or why I thought my mother would be the one to doctor him. Call it the feeling you have when the ocean suddenly becomes too wide. You wish, even if only for a second, you were back on land with the green hills around you and the trees and the safety of the houses with their thatched roofs and chickens in the yard. Dreams, so many dreams.

The day, six weeks later, when Gregory proposed to my mother, I went over to Ellis's to tell her the news. She was down on the floor of her apartment on her hands and knees waxing the hardwood. The smell of the lemon-scented wax made me horny. I got down on the floor and began waxing beside her.

"My mother's getting married," I said. I wanted to grab Ellis right there and have her on the wet, shiny wood.

"Mory!" she said. "That's wonderful!" She was stroking the floor in circular motions. I wanted to tell her she should be going with the grain.

"Is it Gregory?" she said. She had met Gregory two weeks after I took him to my mother's house and had liked him right away. He called her The Duchess.

"They're getting married where I work," I said. I was hoping for some sympathy. I thought it was a lousy idea that would embarrass the hell out of me. Imagine your own mother in her wedding dress getting stuck a hundred feet up and frozen with terror inside the Statue of Liberty while a gray, tufted pirate in a tuxedo screams in six different languages for someone to save her. And that's if things went well.

"Oh, that's a wonderful idea," Ellis said. "Just think what a picture it will make. Think how proud Gregory will be."

Set the starboard on fire, matey, and board her through the smoke.
"What about me?" I said. "What's everybody at work going to say?"

"They'll love it, too." Ellis dropped her waxing cloth and gave me a big wet kiss. Then she tore off my shirt and threw me on my back on the floor.

"Wait a second," I said. But it was no use. She bit my neck and jerked my belt so hard getting it loose that I thought she'd given me a hernia. The new wax squeaked on my backside.

There have been over a thousand weddings at the Statue of Liberty. No rice is allowed; it would feed the rats. Most people have the ceremony out on the grounds or on the wide observation deck. My mother wanted to have it at the very top, inside the head, where you look out through the crown. "It's ridiculous, Mama," I told her. I described the mass of people squeezing to get a look through the tiny portholes. "It's like having a wedding below decks in a slave ship," I said. But my mother had heard Gregory's story of his night swimming ashore, how he was drawn by the lights shining up on the proud head above the water, and, for her, the tight circular walkway with its row of scarred windows looking to the bay became a church.

So here I am, at the highest landing watching her in her white gown going up the stairs ahead of me. Ellis is behind her. The maid of honor. And then Gregory in a black tuxedo that makes him look like European royalty. When he jumped ship that night ten years ago, it was this island that he swam to with his oilskin bag of fresh clothes, thinking if he made it here they would have to accept him. In the morning, no one understood him when he asked for asylum. They thought he was just another tourist and pointed to the ferryboat.

Then, behind Gregory, there's me. I'm going to give away the bride. Sturgis is the best man. The priest is up in front of us all, Father McDougal from the Holy Mission of Saint Bonaventure.

It's going to be crowded up in the Lady's head. All the tourists will be waiting. It will have to be quick.

Ellis is overjoyed. She says now nothing can stop us. Marriage. Should a pirate get married? A girl in every port. What's the use if you marry them all? You have to remember too much that way.

Now, we're at the last landing on the top, before the stairway squeezes up through the neck into the head. A dozen Pakistanis are jammed ahead of us and a dozen more behind. Somehow our party got in the middle of their group. The ones ahead of us are looking back and laughing and pointing. At us? At the others? I'm a stranger in my own country.

But wait. I'm a pirate. I don't have a country. No mother, no father, no wife. Or if I have one, I have a hundred. A mother and a father and a wife down every alleyway. *I'm home, Mama.* Knife between the teeth. She's sleeping in the bed like an innocent baby, like a statue. The hair I pull back. The neck I expose.

My mother smiles and flips her hair, adjusting her veil. We're nearly to the top and she hasn't panicked. Gregory, I'm not so sure about. His knuckles have whitened where he grips the railing. "Gregory," I say, "don't look down."

It's too late. The first Pakistanis are gone into the head now, and my mother sweeps in a white triumph to the top of the stairway. Behind her, we're stopped. The priest's carbon hair looms over her shoulder and he motions to Gregory and calls him, but Gregory isn't paying attention. He won't look up, only down. His face is white, and his pale blue eyes are huge.

There comes this moment in every man's life. You've been sending them down the plank and over the edge all your life, and then one day you step out on it yourself, just to see what it feels like. The water below is so clear and deep. You can see the quick shapes of a few dolphins darting around way down where they've been following the shadow of the ship. You get down on your hands and knees on the plank and you hold on tight. It's freshly waxed and smells of lemons. The ship is rocking more wildly than it has in any storm. You've lost your legs.

"He looked down," I say. Father McDougal's eyes suddenly focus past me, into the deep dark well of the body. His face, too, goes blank. O ye of little faith. Should I hold out my hand, or let him sink?

I look at my mother. She has fear in her eyes now, and I can tell it's spreading. The Pakistanis behind us are getting restless. I turn back and can see them looking down. Oh no, I think, this is the worst. I saw it happen once before with a Boy Scout troop from Alabama. Their leader went first, then, a whole stair load of merit badges white-knuckled to the rail.

Father McDougal is clutching my mother's arm. His gaze is still fixed on the deep canyon of the torso. But Mama has reached around Ellis to get her other hand on Gregory. He won't let go of the railing.

"Gregory," my mother says, "don't think about it. Try to remember your vows."

Ellis is pressed against the railing by my mother's arm and is struggling to keep her balance. Then I remember the oldest pirate trick in the book. I reach up to Gregory's waist and tickle him.

At first he continues his low whimper. Then the huge voice breaks out. The laughter rings down the hollow metal insides of the statue. It's as much of a roar as a laugh, and his hands come free from the rail. My mother's face breaks, too, and she begins to laugh. Ellis is laughing, and behind me I hear Sturgis laughing, and then the Pakistanis. I can even hear laughter from way down below where I can't see the people. The whole inside of the Statute of Liberty is laughing. I wonder if they can hear it outside, across the lawn and the island. Out on the docks where the ferries are loading. Across the water in Battery Park and farther into the city.

We move quickly into the Lady's head. We crouch around the little windows that look out onto the harbor and the tall masts of the city. The wedding is over before I know it.

Who was the first pirate? Some say it was Noah. I prefer thinking it was a swimmer in the flood, paddling along. There sails the Ark. He swims to it, catches on. Knife between his teeth, he climbs up and through a porthole. Incredibly, not even God sees him as he hides, among the beasts and the birds and all the creeping things, waiting for the right moment. They say that pirates shouldn't get married, that they are too bloodthirsty to stay still for long. But I say that a pirate can do what he wants. Sometimes you have to hide, you're outnumbered, you'll wait for your chance. Other times, you walk to the end of the plank, look down into the water, smile, and then jump. Ellis and I will be getting married soon. And I'll still be a pirate even though I may not have a ship. It's a free country after all. The Statue stands in the entrance to the harbor. You can see it for miles. It's laughing. Can you hear it? Sturgis?

THE END

JOHN BENSKO is the author of three books of poetry: *Green Soldiers* (winner of the Yale Series of Younger Poets Award), *The Waterman's Children,* and *The Iron City*. He lives in Memphis, Tennessee, and teaches in the MFA Writing Program at the University of Memphis.

Sea Dogs was set in Apollo, a typeface
designed by Adrian Frutiger in 1962.
Interior text design by Wendy Holdman.
Composition at Stanton Publication Services, Inc.
Manufactured by Bang Printing on acid-free paper.